DEAD BY SUNDOWN

After five years Mike Donohue tracks down his wife's killer, Galen Benitez, to the region known as the Cauldron. Here, Mike meets Lucy Reynolds who is searching for the lost city of Entoro, rumoured to have streets of gold. As Mike suspects that Galen might also be there treasure seeking, he helps her. Up against Galen, and now Lucy's deadly jealous admirer, Mike will need his six-shooter to ensure that he isn't the one who is dead by sundown.

Books by I. J. Parnham
in the Linford Western Library:

THE OUTLAWED DEPUTY
THE LAST RIDER FROM HELL
BAD DAY IN DIRTWOOD
DEVINE'S LAW
YATES'S DILEMMA

I. J. PARNHAM

DEAD BY SUNDOWN

Complete and Unabridged

LINFORD
Leicester

First published in Great Britain in 2006 by
Robert Hale Limited
London

First Linford Edition
published 2006
by arrangement with
Robert Hale Limited
London

British Library CIP Data

Parnham, I. J.
  Dead by sundown.—Large print ed.—
Linford western library
  1. Outlaws—West (U.S.)—Fiction
  2. Western stories
  3. Large type books
  I. Title
  823.9′2 [F]

  ISBN 1–84617–510–0

Published by
F. A. Thorpe (Publishing)
Anstey, Leicestershire

Set by Words & Graphics Ltd.
Anstey, Leicestershire
Printed and bound in Great Britain by
T. J. International Ltd., Padstow, Cornwall

This book is printed on acid-free paper

1

Beyond the next outcrop the buzzards were circling.

With a hollow feeling growing in his gut Mike Donohue hurried his horse on and rounded the outcrop at a gallop. And sure enough, ahead stood an abandoned stage, horseless and incongruous on the otherwise deserted plains.

Mike slowed, running his gaze across every rock and gully as he searched for the attackers, but the only movement came from the buzzards and the drifting shadows of these messengers of death.

Closer to, Mike saw the bodies.

One man lay on the seat of the stage, his head thrown back, gunfire having converted his chest to a bloodied wasteland. A second body dangled upside down from the seat, the arms swaying in the breeze as an entangled leg trapped the body in this undignified position. And from the bullets that had mashed his face to an unrecognizable pulp, Mike reckoned that whoever had raided this stage had fired into this man for long after he'd died.

These two men had been the lucky ones.

When Mike pulled open the doors, frozen grimaces of anguish beyond bearing confronted him, confirming that the man and woman inside had provided the raiders with lengthy and ugly entertainment before they died.

'Galen Benitez,' Mike whispered to himself, uttering the name of the only man who was cruel enough to have perpetrated this senseless atrocity.

One last time Mike strode round the stage, ensuring he missed no details. The flies had found these bodies, but the buzzards had yet to start feasting and that meant he was just hours behind his quarry, perhaps less — the closest he'd been in two years.

With his stride assured he headed for his horse. But then he heard a noise — the barest shifting of pebbles, the sound almost lost in the wind.

He tensed, but avoided looking towards the direction of the sound and instead turned to face the stage. He rubbed his chin and cocked his head to one side, feigning an interest in something in the stage, then paced around it again. But when he reached the other side he slipped his gun from its holster, then threw himself to the ground.

On his belly he fast-crawled beneath the stage, then lay flat. Behind a wheel he thrust his gun out as he stared at the tangle of rocks from behind which the sound had come.

Long minutes passed with the sound not repeating itself.

With Galen getting further away with every heart-beat Mike was considering whether he'd been mistaken, when he saw a flash of a red shirt as a man glanced up from behind the rocks.

In the man's brief appearance Mike saw that this person was shaking, but he still stayed on his belly beneath the stage.

'You over there,' he shouted, 'show yourself.'

Mike listened to the breeze rustle by. When a minute had passed and still no answer had come he spoke again.

'I'm guessing you're one of the survivors. But you got ten seconds to come out or I'll assume you're with Benitez's raiders. What's it to be?'

'I ain't no raider,' a wavering voice shouted. 'I ain't. I ain't.'

'Then stand up and prove it.'

The man who stood was young, perhaps eighteen and, from his hunched posture and shaking limbs, Mike judged that he represented no danger. So Mike rolled out from under the stage and gestured for him to approach.

The young man opened his jacket and turned on the spot to show that he didn't carry a gun. Then, in a tentative voice, he volunteered that he was

Patrick Hancock.

Mike shared his name then gestured back at the dead men. Patrick followed his gaze, winced, then lowered his head.

'All dead?' he whispered.

'Except you.' Mike lowered his voice. 'And I ask myself why.'

Patrick shuffled from foot to foot.

'I ain't proud of myself, but I ran when the shooting started.'

'And you're telling me that Galen Benitez didn't come after you?'

'I am.' Patrick shrugged. 'I figured he was enjoying himself with the woman and . . . ' Patrick snuffled ' . . . I wanted to help, but I reckoned there wasn't much of anything I could do.'

Patrick looked up, his beseeching eyes imploring Mike to speak and perhaps provide absolution for his cowardice, but Mike sneered.

'There was. You could have died.' Mike paced sideways to his horse, ensuring that he still watched Patrick.

'And what do I do now?'

'Don't care.'

'But you got to get me to safety.'

'I got to do nothing. Green Springs is eighty miles that-a-way.' Mike rolled into the saddle then pointed down the trail. 'It'll be one hell of a journey, but on the way you might work out what you did wrong back here.'

Patrick looked down the trail, then in the direction towards which Mike was turning his horse.

'You're not heading to Green Springs. That mean you're going after those raiders?'

'Sure am,' Mike grunted, then glanced at the jagged peaks to his side that surrounded an area known as the Cauldron and towards which Galen had been heading.

Patrick stood tall, a flash of fire in his eyes.

'Then take me with you. The raiders only ran off the horses and we can round one up. This Galen Benitez couldn't have gone far and — '

'And I ain't taking you with me. I don't need no . . . '

Mike looked away, deciding that despite the contempt he felt for Patrick's failure even to try to take on Galen, this young man didn't need to hear that contempt. He shook the reins and hurried his horse on.

'You got to,' Patrick shouted after him, 'because I know where Galen has gone and it ain't where you're heading.'

Mike yanked back on the reins and leapt down from this horse. With his fists clenched, he advanced on Patrick.

'Where?' he grunted.

'I . . . ' Patrick murmured, backing away. 'I won't tell you unless — '

'You will tell me,' Mike roared, breaking into a run. He pounded the last few paces and threw out a hand to grab Patrick's collar, then pulled him up tight to his face. 'Or I'll make what Galen did to those people in the stage seem like a night in paradise. Now, tell me!'

'I can't,' Patrick screeched. 'I got to — '

Mike slapped Patrick's cheek, rocking his head one way, then slapped his face the other way. But then anger got the better of him and he slugged his jaw, sending Patrick reeling.

'One more chance,' Mike snapped, looming over Patrick. 'Or I'll tear you apart with my bare hands.'

Patrick looked up, fingering his jaw. A blaze of defiance consumed his eyes.

'I *can* tell you, but the directions are lengthy. You might — '

'Why, you . . . ' Mike grunted while advancing on Patrick with his fists raised ready to pummel his years of frustration out on this man.

Patrick back-crawled away, but just as Mike loomed over him the realization hit Mike that Galen was getting further away with every second he wasted here. He lowered his fists.

Patrick gulped as he considered Mike's less belligerent stance, then rolled to his knees.

'I will help you,' he murmured. 'But I just want a way out of here.'

'All right. I guess we'd better round you up a horse.' Mike indicated that Patrick should get to his feet, but then glanced at his fist. 'But if you don't get me to Galen by sundown, I *will* tear you apart.'

2

Mike wasted only half an hour in finding a horse for Patrick to ride.

Patrick then wanted to bury the bodies before they moved on, but Mike's fierce glare and another reminder of the urgency of their pursuit silenced him, and they hurried away from the scene of the massacre. But despite Mike's irritation at wasting so much time, he discovered that Patrick was more use than he'd expected.

Although Mike knew Galen's general direction, he'd aimed to take a route via Last Hope, a frontier town on the edge of the Cauldron, but Patrick claimed he had better information and directed him through a winding pass.

And if Patrick did know where Galen's final destination was, Mike now had a good chance of catching him and completing his five-year quest.

'What you going to do when you find this Galen Benitez?' Patrick asked, breaking their silence.

As an answer, Mike just snorted.

'Arrest him?' Patrick persisted. 'Take him to the law and claim the bounty? Try to — '

Mike took a deep breath. 'You talk too much.'

'Yeah, I've heard that, but I don't reckon as I do. I reckon I just talk — '

'Be quiet!' Mike swirled round in the saddle and glared at his new companion until he lowered his head. Then he turned to face the front. 'When you ride with me, even for an hour, you're silent.'

For a full minute Patrick reigned in his exuberance, then coughed.

'If you ain't planning on arresting Galen, why are you after him?'

Mike winced as he weighed up whether he'd gain by answering this talkative young man's question. But despite seeing the potential in probing Patrick for details of what he knew about Galen's destination, even voicing his obsession might diminish the anguish that was his constant companion.

And until Galen was dead, he didn't want to lose that pain.

Five years had passed since he had made the fatal mistake that had made killing Galen Benitez his sole aim in life.

And it had all started over the seemingly minor decision to move a boulder.

Mike had owned 200 acres of farmland near the peaceful Kansas town of Prudence. On the edge of that land there had stood the boulder.

For three years he'd ploughed around it while dreaming up elaborate schemes to move it. Sometimes he dug around it so that he could try to roll it into the creek. But no matter how far he dug down, there was always more rock to uncover and the boulder just sat there, defying him.

Occasionally he chipped away at it, or slipped a lever beneath it and strained, but the boulder didn't move. Increasingly he came to view that boulder as something whose existence stood for more than just an irritating obstacle in his path.

Stella didn't understand his obsession, and perhaps it was his wife's apathy that made him so determined. The boulder was his project and, no matter what anyone else thought, he would damn well find a way to shift it if that were the last thing he did.

And so, one fine late-summer day when the sun filled his heart with harvest cheer, he completed his daily chores early and the long afternoon stretched ahead of him. And that day felt like it was the day when he'd finally move the boulder.

And he did. It took three levers, both oxen and a complicated pulley system that would have impressed Richard Jordan Gatling himself. But as the possibility of the boulder finally moving grew, he became excited. And he got careless. So, when the boulder rolled for its first and last time, it took him by surprise.

That one moment of stunned shock meant he didn't move out of the way fast enough and the huge bulk crushed his leg between the lever and the ground. His leg snapped like a twig, the sound deep and sickening.

For hours he lay writhing and screaming, unable to free himself.

For days he cursed himself as Doc Malloy gritted his teeth and tried to convince him that he wouldn't lose the leg. And it did mend, but as he hobbled around, with annoyance and pain and embarrassment vying for his attention, he wasn't fit enough to help bring in the harvest.

Other homesteaders rallied around and helped Stella, but with unseasonal rain making the task even harder, it looked as if they'd face a harsh and hungry winter. And all because of his foolish obsession.

But then Galen Benitez rode into town, looking for work.

The rough-clad itinerant sported a permanent grin that spoke of his utter contempt for his fellow-man and his bulging eyes appeared to size up everyone he met. And the cold malice in them suggested that the result of that sizing up wouldn't be enjoyable for his victims.

Stella took an instant dislike to him and, as Galen boggled and leered at her, Mike almost sent him on his way. But he had to admit that despite his misgivings he had no choice but to employ this unpromising worker.

Despite his initial concern, for three weeks Galen did everything expected of him. Neither Stella nor Mike warmed to him but, with the harvest coming in, a begrudging acceptance of his position grew. But then, with just a day's work remaining before they could release him, neither Stella nor Galen returned from the fields at the end of the day.

By sundown, Mike was hobbling across his land, calling out to her.

He didn't find her that night, and it

was only when he fetched help the next day that he found her.

By a terrible coincidence she lay back against the very same boulder that had forced him to employ Galen in the first place. She was dead, strangled, the reason for the murder all too clear in her dishevelled clothing.

And Galen was long gone.

The townsfolk searched for him, lawmen arrived, then left; the occasional word drifted back that they hadn't found him but that they were still searching. But Mike was oblivious to everything but getting his leg fit enough to chase after Galen himself.

Sooner than he should Mike mounted his horse and rode off.

And now, after five years of searching, he was just hours behind Galen, perhaps minutes.

But Patrick had asked him a question.

Mike glanced at the sun as it dipped towards the distant mountains. Then, with a harsh smile twitching the corners of his mouth, he fixed Patrick with an icy stare.

'Galen Benitez murdered my wife,' he said. 'I intend to kill him.'

After hearing five years of pain summed up in those few terse words, Patrick was mercifully quiet.

Mike couldn't tell whether his constant prattle was a nervous reaction to the terrible things he'd witnessed, or whether it was his normal nature, but he was relieved to ride quietly and so leave his mind free to hone his plans for what he would do when he found Galen.

Presently the sun winked out of existence behind the mountains. Mike heard Patrick's pronounced gulp and saw him draw his horse back, but Mike had to admit that even if Patrick hadn't got him to Galen by sundown, he had been useful enough to avoid the promised beating. He didn't mention this, preferring to keep Patrick subdued.

And as they rode out of the pass and faced the barren terrain of the Cauldron Mike felt as if he was so close to

Galen that he could see him sighted down the barrel of his gun. He licked his lips with anticipation and resolved, as he did at the start and end of every day, that Galen Benitez would be dead by the next sundown.

But then a gunshot echoed ahead, the sound close.

Mike didn't even glance at Patrick as he spurred his horse on. He heard pounding hoofs as Patrick galloped after him, but he didn't look back as he surged out from the pass and on to the plains. The landscape opened up to him, and before him was a scene of which he'd only previously seen the aftermath.

Gun-toting riders were circling a smaller group. These people had found decent cover behind a sprawling mound of rocks and were returning fire, but with over a dozen riders circling, the attackers were easily pinning them down.

Mike hurried on, his gaze darting between each of the riders. Their forms were too distant for him to discern who they were, but he searched for only one man — Galen Benitez.

Two of the riders broke off from their circling and nudged their horses towards Mike, but a loud voice from the group shouted them back, the voice too distant for Mike to confirm whether it was Galen's.

Still the men wavered but, from the back of the group, riders, one by one, peeled away from their assault, then headed off into the open plains. And, at their front, Mike saw the unmistakable form of Galen Benitez. A life lived constantly on the move had converted his form to a wiry frame and Mike reckoned he could see grey hair poking out from beneath his hat, but it was Galen all right.

With blind anger fuelling him Mike spurred his horse on.

To his side the defenders hurried Benitez's raiders on their way with a burst of gunfire, then hailed Mike. Mike didn't acknowledge them as he galloped past the sprawl of rocks and carried on. With each galloped stride, he closed on the line of riders. Galen was at their front and Mike heard him shout orders. He heard sufficient words to understand that Galen was ordering his men not to fall back but to stay and defend him.

But the backmost rider must have realized the ridiculously unbalanced nature of this pursuit, with one man chasing down more than a dozen. This man pulled back on the reins and turned to face the advancing Mike, who tore out his gun and took careful aim at him, the first obstacle for him to dismiss before he killed Galen.

This encouraged another four men to slow to a halt, then to head back, spreading out as they approached.

The mad fury that had overcome Mike the moment he'd espied Galen still burned in his blood as he advanced on the riders, but in one flashed moment of sanity he saw that he was heading towards five men. And all these men were ruthless enough to have bettered the stage's defenders and others before.

Risking dying at these men's hands while Galen was galloping away would never achieve his sole aim in life. So, with deep reluctance, Mike pulled back on the reins, halting his horse.

Over fifty yards of dirt he stared at the line of five riders, each man sitting impassive and rigid. Then he looked over their shoulders at the fleeing Galen.

He fired overhead, the shot forcing Galen to look back and, with that being the extent of the victory he could hope to accomplish today, he dragged his horse around and hurried away.

The raiders blasted off a volley of gunfire and two men even chased after him, but their pursuit was half-hearted and they relented before Mike had the defenders in his sights.

By now Patrick had joined the group, who had emerged from their cover. Mike saw that there were three of them, a woman and two men. The tallest of the men was shouting encouragement at Mike to join them, but instead, Mike watched the fleeing riders disappear into the spreading dusk.

Hunched forward in the saddle, he debated whether he should join the group or pursue Galen. But under the cover of darkness Galen could lay traps for a pursuing man; moreover, Patrick had not told him what he knew about Galen's destination. So he turned his horse, and as he headed to the group he promised himself that now he was close to Galen he wouldn't lose his trail again.

And next time he would confront Galen on his own terms.

When he reached the rocks the taller of the men offered his name as Roscoe Woods, his companions being Tyrone McColl and Lucy Reynolds.

'Sure am obliged you arrived when you did,' Roscoe said.

'Just luck,' Mike grunted.

'Patrick's told us about you. I reckon

you got quite a tale there.'

Despite accepting that the talkative young man would have struggled to keep quiet for even a few seconds, Mike flashed a harsh glare at Patrick.

For his part Patrick shuffled closer to Lucy and murmured something to her. From the friendly pat on the shoulder that Lucy provided to Patrick and the flashed smile Patrick returned, Mike deduced that Patrick knew her.

'It is,' Mike muttered, 'but not one I chose.'

'I guess not.' Roscoe gestured at the rocks. 'I didn't plan for us to stay here for the night, but it's a good place to make camp. You're welcome to join us.'

Mike nodded. He rolled from the saddle then settled his horse and himself down for the night. He ignored Roscoe's offer to share a meal and instead ate his own food. Then he sat back from the camp-fire that Roscoe had lit. With a blanket drawn up to his chin he leaned back against his saddle and considered these people.

Patrick bustled around, repeatedly glancing at him as he probably searched for a way to encourage him to join the group, while Lucy and Tyrone watched him with the weary suspicion of people who were unused to travelling and the short-term meetings that such a life provided.

Only Roscoe displayed any confidence. And it didn't surprise Mike when he wandered over to him and explained that he was a scout from Last Hope. Apparently Lucy had hired him, Roscoe being one of the few people who was prepared to go into this barren land.

Furthermore, Patrick had been due to join Lucy, and she had been awaiting his arrival in Green Springs. It was only because Patrick had been a week late in joining her that she had headed off without him.

None of this interested Mike, but as the cold of the night descended he relented from keeping his distance and joined the others beside the fire. Patrick welcomed him in with a few murmured platitudes but, aside from returning a nod, Mike didn't join in with their conversation. Instead, he lay on his back and shuffled his hat over his face, feigning sleep.

Although Patrick was wont to prattle, Lucy and Tyrone talked with a quiet and easy familiarity. If he hadn't decided he would keep watch tonight their soft tones might have lulled him to sleep.

Only when the conversation drifted towards Patrick's suspicion about Galen's destination did Mike prick up his ears. But as these people knew each other they didn't need to explain themselves, and Mike didn't learn either their or Galen's destination.

So he flicked his hat back on his head and stood, then paced to the camp-fire. The conversation petered out as all four people watched him.

To avoid using the confrontational approach that had failed with Patrick, Mike took a deep breath before he spoke, the act helping him to fight down his irritation.

'As I moved Galen on,' he announced, 'I'd be obliged if someone would tell me where he's heading.'

'It's a long story,' Lucy said, speaking to him for the first time.

Mike looked at her through the firelight, seeing in the flickering light the hint of something, perhaps sadness, in her downcast gaze.

'I've always got the time to hear about Galen.'

'And I don't want to talk about him.' She bunched a fist and pounded it on a raised knee. 'The damage that a man like him could cause makes my blood boil.'

'The damage Galen has already caused makes my blood boil every day,' Mike snapped, his anger rising despite his attempts to curb it.

Tyrone shuffled on to his haunches, perhaps readying himself to defend Lucy if Mike continued to display his anger, but Lucy rocked her head from side to side, seemingly unconcerned.

Mike took her action as her debating whether to speak rather than her refusal to speak, but it was Patrick who spoke.

'I guess I can't keep it from you,' he said, 'now that you got me to where I was heading in the first place. Galen stole my father's map from my baggage in the stage. He died three months ago, so I thought I'd join this expedition in his memory and — '

'Patrick,' Mike muttered, swirling round to confront him, his fists opening and closing, 'I'll listen to stories about Galen, not about you. So, quit rambling on and tell me where Galen is heading.'

'To Entoro,' Lucy said, looking up and meeting his gaze. It might have been the firelight, but her eyes burned with an intensity that shocked Mike into temporary silence.

'Entoro?' Mike said eventually, his tone now soft. 'Where's that?'

Lucy pointed over her shoulder, the thrust of her arm vaguely indicating a general direction in the darkness.

'It's an ancient city, built hundreds of

years ago by a people who no longer exist.'

'Why would anyone go there?'

She snorted. 'If you have to ask, I can't answer.'

Mike rubbed his chin. 'It'll come down to the usual thing — money. Is something in this ancient city valuable?'

Lucy shook her head, her eyes blazing, then rolled to her feet and flounced away to stand ten paces from the camp-fire.

Roscoe snickered and looked up at Mike, grinning.

'Some have said,' he murmured, his voice containing a mocking note of mystery, 'that this ancient city has streets that are paved with gold.'

Mike turned his gaze on Roscoe, then snorted.

'And you believe that?'

'Of course not.' Roscoe winked. 'But she does and she's paying for my services.'

Tyrone grunted under his breath then jumped to his feet to join Lucy. He raised a hand to place it on her shoulder, but then clutched it behind his back.

'And why are they so upset?' Mike asked, lowering his voice.

Roscoe also lowered his voice.

'Lucy's husband devoted his life to finding Entoro.'

Mike caught the inference in his low tone. He glanced at Tyrone's hunched back, reassessing his initial assumption of his relationship with Lucy.

'And now he's dead?'

'Who is to say? All Lucy knows is he left one day to find this ancient city and he didn't return.'

'I know,' Lucy said, her voice cracking and betraying a depth of emotion from unbearable loss to pride. She swung round then paced back to the fire. 'Holman knew where Entoro was and he found it, and I will find his body and prove that he died after achieving his life's ambition. Then nobody will scoff at his beliefs again.'

Mike maintained a respectful silence

before he replied.

'I wasn't scoffing at the memory of your dead husband. But I don't reckon Galen is stupid enough to believe a story about an ancient city with streets that are paved with gold. He won't go there.'

'And I hope that he hasn't.' She sat, cross-legged. 'I don't want him desecrating the site because of a ludicrous story about gold.'

Mike glanced at the night sky, then shrugged.

'And I hope he does go there, because then I can kill him.'

Lucy opened her mouth to reply, but then closed it and shuffled round to turn her back on him. With only a curt acknowledgement to the others she retired for the night. After the harshly spoken words even Patrick stayed quiet.

The group busied themselves with settling down. Although nobody discussed the arrangements for the night, Mike took it upon himself to take watch. He knew Galen, and although he'd run from him, he could return.

But all was quiet until, three hours into the night, Tyrone stirred and joined him, offering with a few gestures to relieve him.

Mike accepted, but before retiring he drew Tyrone aside.

'You don't exactly strike me,' he said, 'as someone who's interested in an ancient city.'

'And what's that matter to a man who only cares about killing Galen?'

'I want to know whether to believe that Galen really is heading to where you reckon he's heading.'

'I guess I can see that.' Tyrone turned to peer at the low moon. 'And to answer your question, I ain't interested in finding no ancient city. But Holman was my cousin and he sure was.'

Mike nodded. 'Are you here for Holman's sake or for Lucy's?'

Tyrone shuffled closer. 'Holman and me had different aims in life, but when he got himself killed out here, I had to help Lucy in any way I could. But I guess I hope that while we're here, we might . . . '

Tyrone flashed a wan smile that spoke of his hopes for a relationship with Lucy with greater intensity than any words ever could.

Mike shrugged. 'Perhaps it'll be hard for her to consider you until she's seen Holman's body.'

'I know, and that's why I intend to search real well.'

'I wish you luck.' Mike turned to head back to his bedding, but glanced round. 'But while you do that searching, keep out of my way. Tomorrow, Galen Benitez will be dead by sundown.'

3

In the morning Mike awoke before sun-up. He promised himself that Galen would die by sundown, this time with greater assurance than normal, then prepared to move out. But he didn't need to chivvy the others on, as they set off with minimal fuss, each person eager to reach Entoro before nightfall.

After five years of tracking Galen, Mike understood Galen's motivations and, after a night's consideration, he knew that Galen wouldn't believe a story about gold in an ancient city. But he also knew that Galen always sought out every opportunity for personal gain and he would have to uncover the truth before moving on. And that meant Mike could close on Galen by accompanying this group to where they believed Entoro to be.

Lucy had a copy of the map that Galen had stolen from Patrick's baggage. With Roscoe's directions they headed to Snake Ridge, the winding and gorge-filled western boundary of the Cauldron.

Mike scouted around from the group and soon found Galen's tracks. They were heading towards the apparent location of Entoro.

Later in the morning Lucy and Patrick rode beside each other and exchanged comments about what they'd find if the map were accurate. Lucy's tone was clipped, only the occasional quaver in her voice betraying the emotion she must feel as she closed in on a place where her husband had disappeared. And Patrick reduced the level of his chatter as he limited himself to offering hopeful comments about what they'd find.

When they stopped to water their horses at a rare brackish watering-hole, the tracks Mike found were fresh and encouraged him to stare at the approaching ridge with growing hope. And when they rode off he continually expected to see Galen and his men appear ahead. But the sun was dipping from its highest point and he still hadn't sighted Galen when Roscoe drew them to a halt.

He laid out the map on the ground, used the sun to align it to the compass points, then fingered the map's features, matching them to the ridge ahead. He declared himself confident that they were heading in the right direction, and the group set off, but this time, Mike rode alongside Roscoe.

'How close?' he asked.

'Thirty minutes,' Roscoe said, pointing to a gorge ahead, its stark sides pitted with caves. 'According to the map, that's where Entoro is.'

'And how many ways are there out of this gorge?'

'Out?'

'Yeah, Entoro ain't exactly going to be paved with gold and as soon as Galen sees that, he'll leave. I want to 'know where he'll go then.'

'The map doesn't say but I don't believe there is another way out of the gorge.'

'That mean you've been here before?'

'I took Holman into the Cauldron when he first came here.'

'And Entoro?'

Roscoe shrugged. 'I didn't stay to find out whether it was here. He didn't pay me for that.'

Mike nodded, then hurried his horse on, not waiting to explain himself to his fellow-travellers.

Perhaps they realized that he was accompanying them only out of a fortuitous shared interest and that he'd leave them at the earliest opportunity, because they didn't shout after him and neither did he look back. Instead, he stared at the approaching gorge, looking out for Galen.

He judged that the last tracks he'd seen were less than an hour old and that meant he would now be able to see Galen emerging from the gorge if he'd decided to leave. And as he hadn't seen him, Galen must still be exploring.

Mike reckoned his chances of killing Galen were greater if he could trap him in the gorge, and he steeled himself for seeing him emerge, but he reached the entrance without a sighting. So he slowed to ride into the gorge at a slow trot, following a sprawl of recent hoofprints.

There was a bend ahead and Mike headed to the side, then dismounted before peering around the bend, but what faced him was just the end of the gorge. It was almost sheer on three sides. Strata were visible and huge boulders littered the rock base. Worse, the area was deserted but numerous caves pocked the sides.

Mike wasted no thought on the fact that Entoro wasn't here as he considered the caves. He judged that if even one of those caves was larger than it appeared from the outside, Galen could have taken refuge and could remain hidden from him. His cautious nature would also mean he'd have people on the look-out. But if he'd moved on Mike could waste valuable hours searching the caves and wouldn't be able to resume his pursuit until morning.

But Galen had headed into the gorge and, as Mike always investigated all the clues he found about Galen's movements, he searched. He soon lost Galen's tracks when they headed on to the solid rock. So, on foot, he circled round to five different caves, each time crawling up to the entrance, then peering in as cautiously as he could.

But increasingly he started to suspect that Galen wasn't here, a feeling he confirmed when he found a zigzagging path that led up the back of the gorge and a line of hoofprints heading along it.

Mike hurried back to collect his horse, but when he returned to ground level, Patrick and the others had entered the gorge.

Tyrone and Roscoe looked at him with their eyebrows raised and Mike shook his head. But Patrick and Lucy were oblivious to this news. Patrick was scurrying from rock to rock, stopping to shake a triumphant fist, then moving on.

'This is it,' Lucy said, spinning on the spot with her arms outstretched while she provided the first smile he'd seen from her.

Despite his pressing need to move on, Mike arced round to walk past her on his way to his horse.

'And what is *this*?' he asked, halting.

She climbed on top of a boulder, swayed a moment, then gained her balance and knelt to slap the rock.

'Entoro — Holman's ancient city.'

'Holman's ancient city,' Mike intoned, glancing around but seeing nothing but rocks, the caves, the gorge walls, the outbreaks of scrubby vegetation.

'Look here.' Lucy pointed at the boulder she was kneeling on, then, with the back of her hand, gently brushed away the fine layer of dust.

Mike joined her and looked at the

boulder, seeing only weathered rock, but when Lucy swirled a finger, tracing an intricate pattern, Mike saw the markings. They were too precise to be anything other than man-made and although faint and weathered, they definitely made a pattern, although Mike couldn't tell what it depicted.

He shrugged. 'Somebody carved in the boulder, but that don't make this heap of rocks no ancient city.'

'It doesn't, but there's more.'

Lucy jumped to the ground then scurried to the next rock. She swiped away a layer of dust, then dribbled water from her canteen on to the rock. This time the swirling pattern stood out in sharp relief, but again, it didn't interest Mike.

But Lucy jumped on the spot, grinning wildly, then dashed to the next boulder and pointed out the patterns she found.

Mike couldn't muster the enthusiasm to follow her and he exchanged bemused glances with Roscoe and

Tyrone. Only Patrick trailed after her, but he was soon trudging along; perhaps the ancient city that wasn't paved with gold was not exciting him as much as it had excited Lucy.

Having wasted as much time as he could spare on these people and their odd mission, Mike headed to his horse. Roscoe joined him.

'Are you sure Galen has gone?'

'I found a trail out of the gorge.' Mike smiled. 'Don't worry. You and your charges will be safe.'

Roscoe nodded. 'What will you do when you catch up with him?'

Mike slapped his holster.

'Fill him with lead until he dies.'

'Why not just sneak up behind him and slit his throat?' Roscoe mimed slicing a knife across his neck. 'It's silent and gets rid of a man quietly and without fuss.'

'I'll do it any way I can — guns, knives, bare hands. But Galen will be dead by sundown.'

Mike turned to leave, but Roscoe

raised a hand, then directed him to look at a patch of sand. With a finger, Roscoe scrawled shapes and, seeing that he was producing a map, Mike hunkered down beside him.

'This is where we are,' Roscoe said, drawing a cross. 'I don't know where your quarry will go next, but if he's interested in gold, he might go here.'

Roscoe drew a wavy line, signifying Snake Ridge, then placed a second cross at the end.

'Why?'

'Because this ancient city may not have been paved with gold, but there is gold in the Cauldron.' Roscoe stabbed at the cross. 'There's a gold-mine at Bone Gulch. It's well-guarded, but there'll be rich pickings available. If Galen's heard about it, he might try his luck.'

Mike nodded. Galen had been heading somewhere in a purposeful manner before he'd found the map, and a gold-mine sounded a plausible destination to him.

He slapped Roscoe's shoulder, then, without looking back to offer a farewell to the others, headed to his horse and rode up the side of the gorge.

On cresting the top he faced the snaking extent of the ridge. It was as Roscoe had indicated and he could see the solid block of the mountain in the distance, which contained Bone Gulch.

One last time he glanced down into the gorge, seeing the four people below. Three were sitting and watching the fourth, Lucy, running around; her squeals of delight were drifting up the side of the gorge.

Then Mike turned and headed on after Galen.

Mike now relaxed, feeling almost giddy. The time he'd spent with the mismatched group was the longest he'd ridden with anyone in his five years of searching for Galen, and he welcomed being free of them and their distraction.

For an hour he rode along the top of the ridge, then headed down into another gorge. On reaching ground level he headed along the side of the ridge at a steady mile-eating pace, towards Bone Gulch.

Within two hours he found a spot where Galen had stopped less than an hour earlier. From the spacing of the hoofprints afterwards, he deduced that he wasn't in a hurry.

Mike was desperate now to hasten on and catch up with him, but Galen was no fool. He would be worried about how close Mike was and that meant he might have laid a trap, or perhaps he had deliberately travelled slowly to let Mike catch up with him.

Mike headed to higher ground and followed the contours of the ridge. His sure-footed horse tramped through the shifting scree, taking more effort than if he was travelling on ground level, but up here he could see what was ahead.

And it was with a palpable shock that when he'd picked his way around a mound he came across a group of men, who had settled down ahead of him.

Mike shuffled back around the

mound, then secured his horse. He returned to the spot where he'd seen the men, then lay on his belly.

From a distance Mike couldn't confirm what they were all doing, but he saw one man unloading wood to build a fire; another was preparing a meal. The rest were bustling around in a way that suggested they were making camp for the night although sundown was around two hours away.

He quickly detected the lanky form of Galen and kept his gaze on him, watching the arrangements he made to secure the camp. He resolved that he wouldn't leave his sight again until he was dead.

He had learned from painful experience how luck could keep Galen from receiving his justice; now he would take no chances.

Five years ago his wife's body had been in the ground for barely a month when he'd ridden off down the trail after Galen.

In a desperate state, he had searched

every saloon and questioned every homesteader, his driving thirst for revenge stronger than any lawman could muster.

And within two months, he found another farmer who had given Galen work, but that man had seen his true nature faster than Mike had and had run him off his land.

Mike had followed Galen's fresh trail and found him sleeping in a ditch. The snivelling man was wretched and footsore and offered no resistance when Mike captured him.

He should have killed the cringing no-good varmint where he lay, but a respect for the law still burned in Mike. He resolved to return his prisoner to Prudence and let everyone else who had cared for Stella see proper justice delivered.

For two weeks he dragged Galen back towards home, but when he was only one day away from Prudence the weariness of being constantly on guard wore him down at last and Galen seized his chance to escape.

Where he went, Mike didn't find out.

He returned home and brooded, eventually resolving that he would find Galen again and this time, deliver justice his way.

He sold his land and went on the trail, searching, always searching, every day that passed only giving him more time to dream up ever more barbarous ways for him to mete out his revenge on Galen.

From time to time he picked up clues: a stray sighting, a suggestion of a crime that Galen might have committed.

But when he did find him it was down to luck.

Although on Mike's obsessive manhunt he made his own luck.

Everywhere that Mike searched he left details about Galen, and eventually a bartender saw him and passed the message on. By the time Mike received it the message was six months old. It was nine months out of date when he arrived but the trail was far less cold than Mike had feared. Galen had been working on the railroad and when Mike reached the head of the tracks Galen had left just a month earlier to pursue a wild scheme to pan for gold.

And so, high in the hills, Mike found Galen and his two fellow-panners.

For a week he watched them, judging his two associates to be decent enough men, and so he resolved to keep them out of his quest for revenge. And he had luck — an argument flared and the panners left Galen, leaving him alone and vulnerable.

Mike savoured the moment. He built a cage to hold his prisoner, laid out his tools that'd make his last hours hell on earth, then jumped him.

Galen pleaded for mercy, but when he saw the fire in Mike's eyes he shrivelled into the snivelling runt Mike had always known he was.

Throughout a long night Mike vented his feelings on Galen, harrying him with tales of what sun-up would bring.

And at sun-up, he got to work.

He'd always doubted whether he could mete out the torture he'd dreamed of delivering, but with the sun came the conviction that he could do it.

But he never got the chance. The luck that had kept Galen from his grasp for three years saved him.

His two fellow-panners returned. They'd found a nugget and were heading off to turn it into dollars.

On finding Galen caged and screaming for mercy, the men read the situation exactly how Mike would have read it and confronted him. Mike barely escaped with his life and when he followed them he found that Galen had repaid the panners' kindness by killing them and stealing the nugget.

Mike resolved that he wouldn't make the mistake of enjoying killing Galen next time. Then he'd finish the job with one well-directed bullet at the first chance he got.

But with Galen's acquiring of the nugget his fortunes changed. He bought protection and surrounded himself with a whole heap of other desperate men.

And confident now, he escalated the level of his crimes. He raided, then moved on, becoming a bandit with a growing price on his head. But with the greater level of Galen's ambition came a trail that Mike could follow and so, every day, he closed on Galen, always closed.

And now he had Galen in his sights.

So, with a thin smile on his lips, Mike stared down the slope. He watched Galen place two men in lookout positions, where they stared down the trail in the direction from which Mike had been travelling. Then Galen placed one man in a position where he could look in the opposite direction.

But that was the extent of his obvious arrangements to secure the camp.

Secure in his elevated position, Mike saw nothing that would stop him sneaking into camp under the cover of darkness and succeeding in his mission.

Galen's every action suggested misplaced confidence and no awareness of the fact that tonight would be his last.

But Mike was just beginning to memorize the lie of the land so that he could pick the best route into the camp in the dark, when Galen gathered three men around him and headed up the side of the ridge.

And he headed straight for Mike's location.

4

Mike didn't question his luck.

He had been close to getting Galen so many times that he was due a stroke of luck and Galen heading towards him was the best example he could have hoped for.

With his body still and his profile small, he stared down the slope, counting down the paces until Galen would be close enough for him to get a clear shot.

But then Galen stopped, stared up the slope, and did an abrupt right turn. He continued upwards, but now he took a route that would take him more than fifty yards to Mike's side.

Mike considered firing at Galen's side, but then bit back his irritation and looked up the slope. He guessed that his quarry was heading to the top of the ridge to see how much further it was to Bone Gulch.

Mike shuffled himself down to stay hidden from Galen as he passed, then crawled back around the mound. Then he jumped to his feet and scurried up the side of the ridge, the boulder-strewn slope hiding him from Galen. His feet pumped and he bent his body double as he fought against the shifting dirt to reach the top ahead of Galen.

And when he poked his head over the summit, he saw the flat top of the ridge, and nobody else was there.

Bent double, he hurried across the top. The ridge was fifty yards wide. To his left was a sheer drop. To his right was the gentler incline up which Galen was climbing.

He headed for the position where he expected Galen to emerge, aiming to take cover behind a large boulder. But ten paces away from that boulder, he saw movement to his side.

Mike swirled round, seeing the heads, then the shoulders of two men emerge as they battled up the last few feet of the ridge. And neither man was Galen.

Both men did a double-take on seeing Mike, then hurried on to the top.

Mike skidded to a halt. He drew his gun and, with his feet planted wide, ripped out a shot that tore into the man on the left's shoulder, spinning him away from the edge of the slope. His cry forced the other man to dive to the ground and another head bobbed up before that man went to ground below the edge.

Mike knew that Galen wouldn't stay to face him and now he'd be hightailing it back down the slope. So he broke into a run, aiming to reach the edge of the slope above the camp and so be in the closest position to the fleeing man.

From the corner of his eye he saw a man leap up. Firing sideways, he blasted that man in the chest, spinning him away. He kept running. On the edge of the slope he slid to a halt.

Galen was twenty yards below him and, as he expected, running for cover, his arms wheeling as he hurtled down the slope.

With a glorious transcendence of triumph arcing through his veins, Mike snapped his gun arm up and took a sight on Galen's receding back.

But as his finger tightened on the trigger pain exploded across his chest, the pounding thud of a bullet from the sole standing man tumbling him to his knees. His forehead crunched into a rock.

With grim determination he righted himself, but found that he could raise his gun only a few inches and, with no control of his body, he keeled over the side of the ridge.

★ ★ ★

Moment by moment, Mike clawed his way back to consciousness.

But with alertness came the pain, lancing into his chest and his eyes.

He had received a glancing wound to the chest, that much he knew, but he couldn't understand the pain in his eyes until he realized that it came purely from his looking into the low sun. He blinked to clear his vision and slowly became aware of his surroundings and that he lay on the top of the ridge.

Five men were standing back from him. Galen was standing before him and about ten feet in from the edge of the sheer drop, the low sun at his back. His form was dark but not so dark that Mike couldn't see the grin on his face and the gun aimed down at him.

Mike scrambled for his gun, but his fingers closed on an empty holster.

'Go on,' Mike croaked, 'shoot.'

'I might.' Galen paced to the edge of the ridge. He stared down the sharp slope, then turned and walked towards Mike. 'But I reckon you have enough life left in you to entertain me, like your wife did.'

'Let me live and I'll kill you.'

Galen laughed, then directed two of his men to stake Mike out on the ground, grinning even more widely as the men paced towards him and taunted him with details of the torture they were about to inflict on him.

But then Galen made the mistake of holstering his gun, presuming that he was now safe and not realizing that Mike didn't care one iota whether he got to live for only one second after Galen had breathed his last.

The only thing that mattered to him was killing Galen.

So, when the approaching men were two paces from him, Mike rolled to his feet. The men lunged for him, but he feigned to the side, half by design, half constrained by the crippling pain that tore into his chest, but his move suggested he was making a break for it. The men followed his feint, but Mike turned on his heel and hurtled across the ground towards Galen.

His quarry was ten paces away, giving Galen enough time to draw his gun, take careful aim, and fire, but not giving him enough time to avoid an anger-fuelled Mike hurling himself at him. Galen's slug tore into Mike's guts, but by then he was in mid-air and a split second later, he slammed into Galen.

The two men went down heavily and rolled towards the edge, the precipitous drop just feet away. But despite the pain racking his body, Mike had a grip of Galen's chest that he wouldn't release until death came to them both.

Galen struggled as he tried to squirm away from his grasp, but nothing could make Mike release him. He held on to him, then encouraged their roll, heading straight for the edge.

In desperation, Galen threw out his arms and legs and stopped their rolling, two feet from the edge and the sheer drop beyond.

'What you going to do now, Mike?' he grunted, lying on his back, a confident gleam appearing as he stared up into Mike's eyes.

'Kill you,' Mike murmured, his strength eroding despite his anger.

Galen snorted. 'And how are you

going to do that? Throw us both over the edge?'

By way of an answer Mike flared his eyes, savouring the moment when he should finally kill Galen; then he dragged him up close in a terminal embrace. With one last burst of energy, he hurled himself to the side.

A scream tore from Galen's lips. Then they plummeted over the side. The drop was around one hundred feet to the jagged rocks below and neither of them could survive.

Mike saw a glorious vision of Galen's wide-open eyes, but then they hit the side of the slope and the force of the collision dragged them apart. The slope was almost perpendicular and they bounced and crunched downwards.

Mike heard and felt bones creak and snap, but he didn't care. With each tumble, he saw Galen falling along beside him, but then they slammed into a projection and rolled along it. Galen hit a wider length than Mike did and they rolled together, but Mike rolled over the side first. He lost sight of Galen.

And then he must have blacked out because when he next became aware of himself, he was lying still.

He felt as though he was in a dream, his body so jarred and numb that he didn't know if he was dead or alive. He ventured a glance around, not daring to move. He couldn't see Galen, but he had to be nearby.

He flexed his muscles, finding that he was aware of all the extremities of his body, even if they returned jagged and sickening bursts of pain. He decided to risk trying to move, but a gunshot ripped into the dirt two feet to his side.

'He's dead, I tell you,' a voice shouted from on high.

'Then he'll make good target practice.' Another shot ripped out.

Without moving his head, Mike rolled his eyes from side to side. He'd come to rest at the bottom of the ridge and ahead there was no cover. Unarmed, with two bullet wounds and at least one broken limb, he couldn't mount a defence against them. So he had to play dead.

He listened to the gunshots crunching into the earth around him, hearing the whine of them before he heard the report. He judged that the shooters were firing from the top of the ridge and that he was out of their range. When he didn't react to their gunfire the shooting petered out. From the irritated comments he heard from above he reckoned they judged him to be dead, after all.

Still, he waited, staring at the short stretch of dirt that was visible to him and enjoying the anticipation of moving and seeing Galen Benitez's dead body.

He counted to 500 and, as no further gunfire had come, he slowly moved his head to the side to look around him. All was still.

Then he shuffled round on his belly to look behind him. Sharp pains announced themselves: from his right leg, from his wounded chest. But these injuries didn't cause him as much pain as his discovery that Galen wasn't close.

He ran the fall down the side of the ridge through his mind and accepted that he hadn't seen Galen after they'd hit the projection about three-quarters of the way down. He looked up at the projection and accepted that Galen must have rolled to a halt on it. That meant that he'd have to climb up there to ensure Galen was dead before his injuries sapped the life from him.

He threw out a hand and clawed himself forward. But when he pushed himself along with his feet, excruciating pain lanced through his right leg. He looked back, seeing the limb jutting to the side at an angle no leg should ever have.

He fought back the nausea and pushed with his other foot. The projection was around thirty feet above him and the slope to it had a shallow angle which, when fit, he would have climbed in a matter of seconds.

Because of his injured state, it was

getting dark when he closed on the top.

Every clawed foot was hard won. Every dragged movement tore pain through his ripped chest and his shattered leg. But he had to see him. For five years, he'd only lived to kill Galen and he'd die happy looking into his lifeless eyes.

The last five feet had the steepest slope of all and he put every last ounce of his resolve into folding himself over the edge. He flopped to a halt, wheezing through his tortured chest, the steady rhythm of the pain bolting through his broken leg screaming at him. Then he looked around the short expanse of the projection.

The area was deserted.

Galen wasn't there.

5

Mike crawled around the projection. He found spots of blood, but also found footprints and they headed up a less steep part of the slope to the top of the ridge.

Galen had survived the fall.

From the scraping nature of the footprints Mike could tell that Galen had been injured. As Galen hadn't headed to the bottom of the slope to check whether Mike was dead, he hoped that he might have been badly hurt. But he couldn't convince himself of that, as Galen's injuries hadn't stopped him climbing.

Whatever had happened, one fact was clear: Galen was alive and so Mike still had a mission to complete. And for a start, he had to reach the top of the ridge.

Full darkness had descended by the

time Mike flopped over the top. The climb had been slow and painful. With only one leg to support him he had to move like a sidewinder, hunched up on his side with the punctured side of his chest topmost, then pushing himself on with his one good leg.

This way, each shove moved him about two feet, but after dragging himself along for a dozen pushes he had to stop to catch his breath before resuming.

Finding himself on flat ground again he speeded up, a bitter elation filling him as he crawled over the top of the ridge. Galen had left him for dead and, despite his desperate injuries, that gave him a bizarre advantage: Galen wouldn't expect him to return to the camp tonight.

And provided he could muster enough strength, he might be able to use that surprise to kill Galen. That elation blossomed when his route across the ridge took him past his own discarded gun. With the comforting weight at his hip he dragged himself on.

But when he edged his head over the side of the ridge to peer down the other side, his temporary elation fled.

The camp was no longer there. By the light of the moon he saw the abandoned area.

He almost gave up then, lying on his belly with his forehead pressed into the dirt, but within him that desperate need to kill Galen still burned. So, with the pain in his leg and side urging him on, he crawled towards the point where he'd originally come over the side of the ridge.

Time ceased to have meaning, his existence contracting to his steady motion of dragging himself on, pausing for breath, then dragging himself on again. When he'd hurried over the top of the ridge he'd covered the distance in less than a minute, but the moon had arced a quarter of the way towards the horizon by the time he reached his destination.

He rolled over the side, but the slope

was greater than he'd anticipated and in the faint light he rolled down the slope. A scream escaped his lips as his broken leg jarred and he threw out an arm to stop his tumbling, but he rolled on.

He must have blacked out because when he became aware of his surroundings again he was at rest. He orientated himself, discovering that he had rolled into the hollow where he'd left his horse.

With hope burgeoning in his heart he looked around, but then flopped on to his back.

His horse wasn't there.

He called out, screaming until his voice faded to a pained whisper, but he heard none of the sounds that he was sure his horse would provide on his hearing his voice. Eventually he accepted that Galen had taken it.

Mike gritted his teeth and crawled from the hollow. His only hope now was to return to Entoro, but it had taken him most of the afternoon to ride here and, at the speed he could crawl, he faced an impossible journey of many days.

He decided to head to the camp first. As the way to it was downhill, it didn't take him as long as the journey to the top of the ridge and the moon was still lighting his way when he dragged himself into the abandoned camp.

Galen's men had left in a hurry, but they had been reasonably thorough in their cleaning up. But he had more luck than he expected after the disasters of the last few hours.

He found an abandoned pot. The spilt remnants of a cold broth had seeped into the ground, but enough remained in the pot for Mike to shovel two handfuls of sustenance into his eager stomach. With the strength this provided him, he searched the rest of the camp and had more luck.

Galen's men had built a fire, but hadn't lit it, and he found a thick bough, about four feet long. With this, he was able to lever himself to a standing position. He also picked out several short lengths of wood and, as the pot's handle had been secured with twine, he was able to fashion the wood into a splint for the straight part of his broken leg.

Light was returning to the eastern horizon when he began his long journey back to Entoro.

Using his crutch as a second leg, he headed on, the pot dangling from his hip and his leg-splint at least providing him with some protection if he were to fall over.

With the food giving him a burst of strength, he achieved a fair walking pace, passing the point where he'd left his horse within minutes. Even so, he doubted his journey would be anything less than several days.

As he was still alive he guessed that the gunshots hadn't damaged him beyond cracking his ribs, although the area around the bullet wounds was too painful to touch and the walking motion repeatedly freed blood that drenched his shirt. But he had no choice but to plod on and on.

Whatever optimism had forced him to gather the detritus from Galen's camp and set off back to Entoro was eroded as the sun rose ever higher. He guessed that he walked for a half-mile before he needed his first rest, but his second foray achieved less than half that distance and with every subsequent effort he spent more time resting and less time walking.

Snake Ridge was beside him and he soon found the prints Galen had made when he'd headed towards Bone Gulch and, later, his own prints. But his recollection of that journey told him that Entoro was in a gorge that was further away than he could see.

He'd passed two other gorges on the way to this place and even reaching the first felt beyond his strength. But with that burning desire to keep going that had fuelled him for the last five years, he stumbled and hobbled along beside the ridge until he reached the first gorge.

The sun was setting by then and although he continued to walk as long into the night as he could, he eventually collapsed and was too exhausted to rise again.

It was light when he awoke. He set off, but with the sun came an unnatural warmth. Sweat poured off him. At the first watering-hole he dug down with his crutch, then flopped on his side before the muddy water and drank until he felt fit to burst, but his thirst remained unquenched.

Then he steeled himself to bathe his wounds. Matted blood had stuck his clothing to his chest wounds and prising the cloth away brought a flesh flow that smelt foul. And the skin around the wounds was taught and shiny.

Even if the bullets hadn't delivered a terminal wound, he guessed that they'd provided an infection and that had given him a fever. His inspection of his leg was more promising, but not much. When he slipped out of his boot he could feel his toes and, although the leg was bent, the skin around the broken leg was clean and undamaged.

Even so, he had to find help before either the erosion of his strength or the fever killed him.

He pressed on through the day, reaching the second gorge as the sun was lowering. By now, his vision was blurred and he had to fight to keep awake. A ferocious headache was pounding in time to the throbbing in his leg and the rhythm started to lull him to sleep even while he was walking.

At this gorge he climbed, following the route he'd taken when he'd followed Galen.

He consoled himself with the thought that he was more than half-way to Entoro, that the top of the ridge was flat and provided a route that was easy to follow.

Night had fallen by the time he reached the top and he hobbled along by moonlight. The chill of the night brought an apparent reduction in his fever and he felt elated enough to play a game with his mind. He told himself that Entoro, and so help, was behind the next rock and that his sole aim in life was to reach it.

And when he reached that rock he picked another rock, told himself that help was there, and headed for it.

As the night wore on, the game stopped being a game.

He started to believe that help really was behind the next rock and his hopes plummeted whenever he discovered that it wasn't, but then soared again when he decided the next rock contained it.

With his hopes rising and dashing, he staggered on.

Deep in the night, he heard a crack as his trusty crutch broke and he tumbled to the ground, but that didn't stop him and he crawled on. He'd lost his pot but that didn't matter now. There was no water up here, but the cold kept his fever at bay more effectively than bathing his brow did.

'Galen,' he muttered to himself, 'you'll be dead by sundown. Galen, you'll be dead by sundown.'

This litany echoed in his skull and constantly reminded him of why he was putting himself through this living hell.

He was still crawling and muttering when daylight returned, but with the light came the heat and the delirium.

In his fevered state, voices and faces came to him: Galen mocked his predicament. Lucy encouraged him to carry on. Strangely, his wife didn't visit him, but he didn't expect her. She was dead and he was alive, but even so, he wasn't sweating any more and he imagined his body to be a dried-up husk.

With his forehead brushing the ground, he studied every inch of his journey, the pebbles like boulders, the grit like rocks, the moss he prised off the ground his only nourishment, the moisture he licked off the cool sides of rocks his only way to quench his thirst.

He couldn't lift his face high enough

to see where he was going, but that didn't matter as much as forcing himself on, ever on.

Tyrone's face came to him and swirled in and out of his vision, then disappeared. Mike thought that it had probably been a dream, a feeling that grew when other faces appeared.

He was on his back. Patrick was looking down at him and Lucy was kneeling beside him, clutching a towel, which she lay over his brow. It was cool and when she removed it she dabbed his parched lips, letting moisture seep into his mouth.

But only when her hand brushed his forehead did he accept that he wasn't suffering a dying man's last cruel dream. He had dragged his way back to safety, but when he asked where he was, nobody reacted, so he guessed that he hadn't made a sound and let merciful oblivion claim him.

He awoke periodically and saw disorientating views of the sky and of the ground. One time, firm hands were dragging him to the side. Another time, they were encasing him in blankets. Then he was bouncing along. He was aware enough to realize that he was being dragged back to Entoro, but he blacked out again and when he came to it was dark, a day passing in a matter of moments.

He was parched, his body desperate for water. He cried out for sustenance, but some part of him told him that his cries only echoed in his mind.

But then a cool bottle pressed against his lips and he gulped the liquid. It burnt his throat worse than the roughest rot-gutting whiskey. He coughed and spluttered, but the bottle wouldn't go away and he drank again.

This time he realized that the liquid *was* whiskey and he was too weak to do anything but gulp it down.

When the bottle left his lips, he lay back and dragged in shallow gasps of air. In his weakened and hungry state, he saw that a cave roof was above him, but it appeared to swim around him.

He remained just conscious enough to realize that it was still dark and that Tyrone had been feeding him the whiskey while Lucy bustled around him. Then Tyrone pressed the bottle to his lips again and he drank until he felt ready to vomit, then shook his head, freeing his lips. Before Tyrone could right the bottle the contents emptied over his face.

'What're you doing?' he grunted, then coughed so violently that pain ripped through his chest.

'It's like this,' Tyrone said, laying a hand on his shoulder. 'You got a broken leg to drag back into place and there's a bullet to get out of your chest. We either do it while you're sober and awake, or while you're drunk and blacked out.'

Mike gulped. 'In that case, get me another bottle.'

★ ★ ★

A new day brought a stunning headache but surprisingly little pain. His leg lay straight and splinted. Bandages, which on closer inspection proved to be a ripped-up shirt, encased his chest, although his saviours had left the area around the wounds open, presumably to help drain away whatever poisons the bullets had dragged into his body.

But the thoughts that resounded in his mind were simple: he was alive, he would mend, and he would kill Galen Benitez.

His weakness would let Galen get some distance away from him, but that didn't matter. He'd lost his trail before and picked it up again.

And this time Galen wouldn't expect a dead man to find him.

From time to time his saviours looked in on him.

Mike returned grateful nods, but devoted the rest of the time to sleeping.

He might have been obsessive in his quest, but he knew when the time for rest had come, and that time was now. After his wife's murder he'd pursued Galen far sooner than he should have done. Later he'd force himself to get fit faster than any normal person would.

But that was for another day.

In the stifling heat of the afternoon he awoke and ate the stew Lucy provided for him, but vomited it all back. But later in the day she arrived with a thin broth. Mike kept this gentler food down and he favoured her with a brief smile when he returned the bowl.

'Thank you for everything,' he said.

She frowned. 'And it was all wasted effort when you're determined to kill yourself.'

Mike flinched. 'I'm not determined to kill myself, only Galen Benitez.'

'And you'll probably die in the attempt.'

'If I have to.'

Lucy headed to the cave entrance, but then stopped and turned to Mike.

'Why?'

'As you once said to me: if you have to ask, I can't answer.'

She provided a smile, then looked outside.

'You're right, but I've lost someone who was dear to me, too. I don't know for sure where he died or how he died. I'd do anything to get him back, but nothing I can do will return him to me.' She turned to look down at him. 'I've moved on. Why can't you?'

'Because I can't,' Mike snapped.

'You can't, and that's why we've wasted our time by saving you.'

'Let me explain then — '

'Don't bother.' With a determined swing of her skirts she swirled round and headed out of the cave.

Mike watched her go, even calling out to her again. He wanted to explain why he had to kill Galen, not the facts that he sometimes revealed, but the feelings that clawed him up inside, the feelings that he'd never told anyone about.

Why he wanted to do that, he didn't know, but she hadn't wanted to hear what he was thinking and, for some strange reason, that hurt him more than he expected.

6

For Mike time passed slowly. He had nothing to occupy his time other than to complete the irritatingly slow task of healing.

Roscoe Woods had left on the same day that Mike had set off after Galen, Lucy only saw him when she changed his dressings and when she brought him his meals, and Tyrone rarely looked in on him. But Patrick visited him several times a day and babbled. Mike used the excuse of his weakness to feign sleep, but that rarely stopped Patrick from talking.

But as soon as he felt strong enough he persuaded Patrick to slip a hand under his arm and lever him to his feet so that he could hobble around the cave.

His injured leg stuck out and he avoided putting any weight on it, but his five-yard excursion cheered him by making him feel that he was returning to health.

Several times that day Patrick helped him on this journey. Each time Mike risked slightly more movement until he understood his limitations.

The next day Patrick returned with a crutch. It was heavy and far too thick, but Mike slapped Patrick's back, then ushered him away to give him room. It took him ten long and painful minutes to work out how he could lever himself to his feet, but he did it and he walked unaided to the mouth of the cave for the first time.

Outside, Entoro had changed. Lucy had circled various areas at the bottom of the gulch with ropes and she had placed stakes in intricate patterns, but Mike couldn't tell what those patterns signified. And from Tyrone's bored expression Mike deduced that he didn't know or particularly care either.

But his arrival was interesting enough to raise a ragged cheer from him and he hurried over to join Mike and offer encouragement.

Lucy looked up at him, shrugged, then returned to leaning over a pad of paper. Mike saw that she was tracing out the pattern on the boulder before her. For some reason he wanted to see what that pattern was. But then Tyrone blocked his view and joshed him with comments about how lazy he'd been.

Mike took his comments with good grace, but as he shuffled round to return to the cave he looked at Lucy again.

She had her back to him.

He shrugged and turned, but not before he noticed that Tyrone was looking at him. When Tyrone saw his interest he too looked down the slope at Lucy with his brow furrowed.

★　★　★

A month after his first unaided walk Mike had mastered the skill of hobbling around Entoro.

As much as he was able he helped with the daily duties, finding in himself a greater desire to help others than he had had at any other time in his quest, but he guessed that that resulted from his gratitude.

Now that he didn't need Patrick's help to get around the young man receded into his shell and neither did he help Lucy.

Despite Patrick's apathy, Lucy was progressing with her documentation of Entoro, but as she estimated that her task would take another three months the time spent here increasingly irritated Tyrone. He spent his time on solitary games of chance and hunting trips, but the stark environment and the sheer dullness of the ancient city let tempers fray whenever he returned.

But Lucy was more even-tempered and she was a natural healer.

One day she declared that the poison had left Mike's body and that his broken ribs had almost healed. His chest still ached, but the broken leg was a more serious problem. The break had been to his bad leg and she reckoned it would take another two months to heal.

Despite the mixed nature of this news, Mike celebrated his steady progress by shuffling out of the gorge for the first time. But when he paused to rest beside a boulder he saw that Patrick was also here and was staring at the plains without moving or showing any sign that he was aware of Mike's presence.

Mike shuffled close enough to see Patrick's glazed eyes before he flinched.

'Didn't mean to startle you,' Mike said.

'You didn't,' Patrick said, his tone vague. 'I was thinking.'

'You not appreciating this ancient city as much as Lucy is?'

Patrick sighed. 'I guess it ain't what I expected.'

'You really thought they'd be streets of gold?'

'I guess not, but I thought it'd be more interesting than . . . than this.'

Patrick waved his arms, indicating the barren gorge. 'I didn't have much interest in what Holman or my father had dreamed of finding, but I had to come. I owed him that.'

'And now?'

'And now . . . ' Patrick sighed. 'Now I'm wondering what I can do next.'

'Sounds to me like you need to get away from this place and find your own path.'

Patrick nodded. 'I am wondering about heading after Galen.'

'That's my quest,' Mike snapped. 'Find your own.'

Patrick pouted. 'I want him to die, too.'

'Killing some people you'd sat with in a stage ain't the same as killing your wife.'

'There's more than just that.' Patrick snuffled, his eyes downcast. 'I acted like a scared child back at that stage and I got to prove that ain't the man I'm destined to be.'

'We all do things we regret. Don't

waste your life over something in the past you can't change.'

'You telling me not to go after Galen?'

'I'm not telling you to do nothing. I'm telling you to find what you want to do, not what other people reckon you should do.'

Patrick nodded then returned to staring at the plains.

Mike hobbled back to the cave for a rest, but when he emerged two hours later he found that Patrick had taken his suggestion to heart. He had headed off to Last Hope, the nearest town, figuring that he had nothing left to achieve here.

With his departure leaving just the three of them, Mike tried to strike up conversations with Tyrone, but Tyrone's sullen state had intensified. He just sat half-way up the side of the gorge and watched Lucy work, the mixture of longing and fear in his gaze conveying that he was her permanent guardian and that somebody was about to attack her at any moment.

With no other distractions available, Mike offered to help Lucy with her work.

She refused, but when he insisted she reluctantly accepted, although she viewed his offer with suspicion and allocated menial tasks to him that only took a few minutes to complete before he had to report back for the next one. But gradually she accepted that he genuinely wanted to help and let him do more, even letting him help in the seemingly endless task of reproducing the patterns on the boulders.

Even with Mike scurrying around, Tyrone didn't offer to help. If anything he withdrew into himself even more.

But in an odd way Mike enjoyed his duties, taking pleasure in Lucy's quiet nature and enjoying being given tasks by a woman in the way that he'd enjoyed Stella's bossing him around on the farm in a former life.

But despite his enjoyment, Lucy always spoke to him using her clipped tone, conveying with her brusque attitude her contempt for his obsession with getting fit enough to pursue and kill Galen.

After another month of steady routine he was stronger, and his daily ritual promises that he would kill Galen by sundown felt increasingly possible. So, when he'd completed his day's duties, he often risked going on longer journeys, sometimes hobbling for miles before returning, tired but satisfied at his growing strength.

But one evening he risked more than usual. He threw down his crutch and resolved to see how far he could walk unaided.

He managed two paces.

He was so eager that he tripped over the smallest of pebbles and came crashing down. He lay, cursing his stupidity and steeling himself for the pain that would announce he'd destroyed months of healing in one foolish moment.

But the pain didn't come, and when he dragged himself back to his crutch and stood he found that his leg was fine. Still shaken up after that failure, he returned to Entoro. But on shuffling back into the mouth of the gorge he couldn't see either Tyrone or Lucy. This was unusual as they usually sat outside to watch the sun set.

Then he heard a scream. It was strangulated and, as it echoed back at him from the other side of the gorge, Mike broke into a hobbling run. His only thought was that Galen had returned and he didn't have his gun, but as he neared the cave he still saw nobody and when a scream ripped out again it came from the cave.

Mike hurried up the slope to the cave with as much speed as he dared and peered inside.

In the middle of the cave Tyrone and Lucy stood facing each other. Tyrone held both of Lucy's hands, but was straining as he tried to drag them together so that he could grasp them both in one of his hands.

Lucy was kicking and squirming, but

failing to wrest herself from his grasp. Tyrone planted a kiss on her lips, but she thrust her head away from him and he had to spin her round before he bent to try to kiss her again.

'Get your hands off her,' Mike grunted, taking a hobbling pace into the cave.

Tyrone ignored him and continued to try to drag Lucy into his arms, so Mike hobbled across the cave, grabbed his shoulder, pulled him away from Lucy, then slugged his jaw.

With all his weight being on his uninjured leg, Mike could deliver only a weak blow, but even that was strong enough to knock Tyrone to the ground.

Tyrone stared up at him, his hurt expression possibly resulting more from surprise than from any pain he was suffering.

Mike tottered to a halt and planted his crutch to the ground to avoid falling. Then, standing on one leg, he raised a fist and stood sideways to Tyrone, while Lucy stared at Tyrone with her hands on her hips and her eyes blazing.

'Get out my sight,' she screeched.

'I can explain,' Tyrone murmured, getting to his feet, 'if you'll just — '

'I've heard everything I need to from you and if I ever see you again, I'll break every bone in your body.'

Mike hobbled along to stand beside her.

'And I'll be holding you down while she does it.'

Tyrone looked from Lucy to Mike, then back to Lucy. He snorted, then swiped his fallen hat from the ground and paced away.

'I'm obliged for your help,' Lucy said, her voice hoarse as she watched Tyrone head through the cave entrance. 'But I can take care of myself.'

'I don't doubt it, but that's still no reason to stand by when a woman is in danger.'

'I guess not.'

Mike looked away from Lucy. 'And was that . . . was that what it looked like?'

She didn't reply immediately as she lowered her head and sighed.

'I think he made his intentions clear.'

Lucy turned her back and flounced away to stare into the short tunnel at the back of the cave. Mike shuffled round to look at her and saw her shoulders shake as a sob shuddered from her lips.

He wavered between going to her and leaving her alone, but as he reckoned that nothing he could say to her would help to mend what could be a terminal rift, he turned and shuffled out of the cave.

At the bottom of the gorge Tyrone had already collected his belongings and was preparing to leave.

'You don't have to go,' Mike called out as he shuffled down the slope towards him.

Tyrone glanced up, his jaw set firm and his eyes watering with hurt and a determination to ignore all advice.

'I have to,' he said, his voice gruff. 'I'm in the way.'

Mike rocked to a halt. 'You're not. Before today Lucy was enjoying your company.'

'But you weren't.'

With this exchange having veered off in a direction Mike hadn't expected, he tipped his hat back.

'What you mean?'

'I mean I've seen the way you look at her. One of us had to win her heart, and I guess it wasn't me.'

Mike raised his eyebrows with genuine surprise.

'You got it wrong. As soon as I'm fit I'm going after Galen, and a woman don't exactly fit into those plans.'

Tyrone looked at Mike, but when Mike met his gaze, he winced and slapped a fist against his thigh.

'Then I made another big mistake,' he muttered. 'And I got to go.'

Mike hobbled on to stand before Tyrone.

'I don't reckon you made that big a mistake. You're a decent man and you wouldn't have forced your — '

'Of course I wouldn't,' Tyrone roared, his voice echoing in the narrow gorge. He took a deep breath, then lowered his voice. 'I lo . . . I wouldn't do that.'

Mike ventured a smile. 'And when Lucy's calmed down, I reckon she'll understand that, too.'

Tyrone glanced up at the cave. 'She won't. She made that clear.'

'You can't change what's just happened, but at least you've let her know how you feel about her.' Mike smiled, trying to instil a lightening in Tyrone's mood, but Tyrone continued to glare at him. 'And after so long wondering whether you should tell her, that's progress.'

Tyrone snarled, but as Mike continued to smile, he returned a brief smile and joined Mike. He paced round to look up the gorge.

'I'll be honest with you, Mike,' he said, his tone level and the anger gone from his voice. 'When I said I made a big mistake, I didn't mean just now, I meant after Holman didn't return. I shouldn't have pursued Lucy. I should have supported her, then moved on, but I thought she'd forget him. But she won't. She's still married to a dead man.'

'After losing someone, everyone heals at a different rate.' Mike lowered his head a moment. 'Some of us never heal.'

'I know that.'

'But perhaps if she finds Holman's body she'll be able to move on.'

'And I know that, too, but you don't understand.' Tyrone coughed. 'I found Holman's body three days after we arrived here.'

'Did you tell her?'

'I intended to when the time was right.' Tyrone patted Mike's shoulder, then turned to his horse. 'But I guess you'll have to do that now.'

7

With just the two of them remaining at Entoro, Mike found himself in a quandary. Every day he became stronger and the day when he could move on came closer.

A week after Tyrone had left his leg pained him no more and he found he could ride one of Lucy's spare horses without trouble. And so his thoughts turned to restarting his quest, but he also devoted a lot of his time to worrying about Lucy.

He watched her and noted that she was self-sufficient in gathering food and water. So he became confident of her ability to survive here unaided.

But despite this he hoped that she would also be ready to move on soon, so that he could leave her in a safer place, like Green Springs.

Every night after dinner he tried to

voice his concerns, but found he could say nothing to Lucy. So, to avoid the uncomfortable silences he scouted around, gradually broadening his expeditions. After another week he steeled himself to enter the highest cave in the gorge where Holman's body lay.

Tyrone had left the corpse where he'd found it, lying five feet in from the entrance to the dry cave and propped against the wall. The locale was remote enough to keep scavengers away and the wind ripping in to the cave was fierce enough to have mummified the corpse.

And even though Mike reckoned Holman had been dead for more than a year, he could see the deep slash wound across his withered neck which had killed him.

It was this discovery that tipped the balance for Mike and forced him to admit that he had to leave.

The next day he didn't help Lucy in the daily tasks or with her work in documenting Entoro, but he found reasons to cross her path and ask whether she was all right.

She replied curtly, but he detected in her eyes a knowledge that he was ready to leave.

But he couldn't make himself say the words. So the day passed without his airing the subject.

It was the evening, and they had finished eating and were sitting in the mouth to the cave when she put down her plate and turned to him.

'You're leaving,' she said.

'I guess I am.' He threw his plate on top of hers and turned to face her. 'And I'd be obliged if you came with me.'

'That mean you're not going after Galen?'

'Of course I am, but I'm heading to Last Hope first to see what I can learn. I can leave you there or in the next town.'

'I won't leave until I've completed Holman's work.'

Mike bit his lip as he debated whether he should tell her the secret Tyrone had left him with, but on seeing the serenity in her expression, he couldn't do that, then leave her.

'Are you hoping that Tyrone will return?' he asked.

'No.' She shuddered. 'He's been here twice before. I don't think he'll return for a third time.'

Mike raised his eyebrows. 'Twice?'

'He came here searching for Holman late last year.'

'He never mentioned that.' Mike shrugged. 'But Tyrone's a decent man.'

'Perhaps, but I'm not so sure.' She frowned. 'Tyrone's not what you think he is. You're a good man, trying hard to be bad, but Tyrone is a bad man, trying hard to be good.'

'I didn't know that.'

'He's Holman's wayward cousin and when Holman died he lost the calming influence in his life. He's tried to stay out of trouble, but I reckon that one day he'll see an opportunity and return to his old ways.'

'Perhaps he needs a different calming influence.'

She nodded. 'He does, but that person isn't me.'

'That mean you're still hoping to find Holman alive?'

'I know he's dead.' Her tone was calm as she looked up and let the breeze rustle her hair. 'But I'm close to him here, almost as if I can hear his voice in the wind.'

'But he's in the past and you can't live your life then.'

She snorted. 'I know that, but I don't know how you can say it. You're the one who's living in the past, forever searching for a man who's always one step ahead of you.'

'Galen killed my wife,' Mike snapped.

'He did, but he's killing *you* every day.'

Mike grabbed a handful of dirt and let it sprinkle through his fingers.

'And completing Holman's work is destroying you every day.'

They sat staring at each other, but Lucy was the first to smile.

'Neither of us can question the other.

We both have to get over our loss in the best way we can. For you, that's killing Galen. For me, that's finishing Holman's work, but I'm doing that out of love. What you're doing, you're doing out of hate, and you can't move on until you put that hate behind you.'

Mike batted his hands free of dirt.

'Like you said — neither of us can question the other.'

'I can. In the last few weeks I've seen the man you once were — a decent man who is kind and gentle, a man who must have made a good husband for Stella. But that man won't be the same man as the one who rides out of here. That man will be gone for ever and the man who'll ride into Last Hope will be the tortured, driven man I first met three months ago.'

Mike gulped, biting back this truth.

'And why do you care?'

The question hung unanswered in the air and as Lucy's gaze softened, Mike noticed for the first time that her eyes were deep blue.

'Is it so hard for you,' she whispered, 'to believe that another person could care about you?'

'Yeah.' Mike gulped. 'I ain't exactly sought out company these last few years.'

'And now?'

Mike cocked his head to the side.

'What exactly are you asking of me?'

Lucy opened her mouth, but then looked away. She breathed deeply, her chest rising and falling, but then swirled round and the arms she threw around his neck and the huge kiss she mashed into his lips said more than any words could offer. She pulled back.

'Does that explain?'

Mike blinked hard, his heart hammering in response to her unexpected action, but then an animal instinct that he thought he'd never experience again took over. He wrapped his arms around her, then pulled her close.

'No,' he whispered. 'Tell me again.'

★ ★ ★

For the last five years, whenever Mike had awoken, he'd enjoyed a few seconds of peace, moments when the reality of his life had yet to intrude on the lethargy of his dreaming world.

But then Galen Benitez always tore into his mind and his single-minded obsession of finding and killing him by sundown governed the rest of his day.

But today the reality that intruded was a different one, a contented and satiated existence where life felt good.

Galen was still there, pressing on his thoughts, but finding him didn't feel as important as enjoying the comforting pleasure of the warm body that lay beside him. Killing Galen wasn't as enjoyable a thought as the ridiculous delight he felt in discovering that his arm had gone numb because another person had lain on it.

After Stella's death he didn't think he'd ever be able to form a friendship with another person, never mind feel the passion he'd felt last night, but he had and he felt no guilt. And come the approaching sun-up, he faced a terrible decision.

But that didn't stop him looking towards the mouth of the cave and savouring Lucy's melodious breathing as if each inhalation and exhalation were her last. He guessed she was awake — her breathing was too controlled — but he also guessed she didn't want to do anything other than share what could be their last moments together, too.

And sure enough, at first light, she raised herself from him and dressed, then padded to the cave entrance to look out. Mike dressed in silence and joined her.

'You're still leaving,' she said, not looking at him.

'Yeah,' he said.

'Is there anything I can say that'll stop you?'

'You said plenty last night.' Mike took a deep breath, admitting something to himself that he hadn't thought he could, until now. 'But I will come back.'

'I might not be here.'

'Then tell me where you'll go.'

She snorted, then turned to face him, her unbound hair swinging.

'And if I don't, you'll still find me, is that what you're telling me?'

'That's the way it is.'

'You're wrong. It may take you years to find Galen and you might die when you do.' She fixed him with her limpid gaze. 'I don't want that to happen. Don't go.'

'I have to go.' Mike gulped, moistening his dry throat. 'I have to.'

'I understand your loss, believe me, but I don't want a man who can kill another. I want to be with the kind and gentle man of the last few weeks. I want to be with the man I knew last night. I don't want to be with a killer.'

'They're the same man.'

'They are, but you're capable of great courage and great compassion. Vengeance shows neither. Leave now, if you have to. But as you head off after Galen, think about what's behind you, not about what's ahead of you. It'll take me another few weeks to finish here.' She looked to the lightening sky, then pointed at the sinking crescent moon. 'Come the next full moon, I'll leave. Either return here by then and we can try to forge a life together, or never return.'

She fixed him with her gaze, then planted a warm kiss on his cheek.

Then she was gone, heading into the cave, and there didn't seem to be anything else Mike could say.

8

The paces to his horse and the journey out of the gorge were the longest Mike had known.

He could have turned back a hundred times, but the obsession that had driven him on for the last five years couldn't leave his heart after just one night.

He wanted to start a new life with Lucy, but he also knew that the knowledge that Galen was alive somewhere would eat him up inside and destroy him. He had to find him, kill him, then come back and find Lucy, wherever she would go.

With that resolution, he hurried on, a new urgency pressing upon him.

He'd lost Galen's trail before but that didn't concern him. His usual technique was to head to the nearest settlement and ask whether anyone had seen him or heard a rumour. This policy always worked because a man like Galen made ripples.

So, two days after leaving Lucy in Entoro, Mike rode into Last Hope.

The town was the nearest settlement to the Cauldron and the squalid collection of shacks appeared to understand their precarious position. The town nestled on the side of a hill, enjoying the full blast of the low sun. To the north the mountains were jagged heaps of impenetrable splendour, ensuring that Last Hope was the last possible place where anyone would want to set up a town.

Aside from the occasional face peering out from the buildings, nobody ventured outside to watch him ride into town.

Mike headed into the saloon, a tent that adjoined the store and which had a board outside that optimistically advertised this place as being the Paradise saloon.

Only one customer was within and

he hadn't heard of Galen Benitez, but he directed Mike to a man who did know about people who had headed into the Cauldron — Roscoe Woods.

And sure enough, outside a rough shack on the edge of town stood a familiar squat horse.

Mike was dismounting when the owner emerged from the shack, did a double-take on seeing him, then hailed him, beaming a huge smile.

'Glad you've finally left that cursed place,' Roscoe said, then peered around. 'Lucy not with you?'

'Nope,' Mike grunted, scowling. 'She makes her own decisions.'

Roscoe nodded. 'Met Tyrone McColl a while back. He reckoned you and her were getting close and that he was in the way.'

'He's entitled to his opinion.'

'If you say so.' Roscoe smiled, raising his eyebrows in apparent hope that Mike would return a smile, but Mike maintained his scowl. 'You still searching for Galen Benitez?'

'As ever.'

'Then I got news for you. I was right about Galen. He's been picking off the miners when they leave the gold-mine at Bone Gulch and try to get to Green Springs. The last I heard, the leader of the miners, Lazarus Heath, was putting together a team to guard the gold when they take it out, and perhaps track him down in the process. I reckon Lazarus is still in Green Springs if you want to find out what he knows.'

'Obliged for the information.' Mike turned and looked along Last Hope's main road, confirming that nobody was outside. 'And the rest?'

Roscoe narrowed his eyes. 'What you mean?'

Mike paced round to stand before Roscoe and tucked a thumb in his gun-belt.

'About you and about the way you suggested I could kill Galen: a knife across the throat.'

Roscoe rubbed his chin as he rocked his head from side to side.

'It's quick and easy.'

Mike nodded and glanced away, but then swirled round and lunged. His grasp closed on Roscoe's throat and he pulled him up close.

'Quick enough to kill Holman Reynolds, was it? Quick enough to kill other travellers you took into the Cauldron, was it? Quick enough to kill Lucy, is it?'

Roscoe struggled, but he found that Mike's grip was firm. He slumped.

'I don't know what you mean,' he bleated.

'You do. You're one of the few men who's prepared to head into the Cauldron, but when you take people in, not all of them come out.'

Roscoe shook his head, his eyes were watering and possibly he was hurt at the accusation. With a snort Mike threw him back.

'You got no right,' Roscoe murmured, loosening his collar, 'to accuse me of that.'

Mike advanced a pace on Roscoe,

but then Roscoe's hand whipped under his jacket. Light flashed as a knife emerged, the blade whipping up in an arc that would plunge into Mike's throat.

But Mike had been wary of the possibility of Roscoe turning on him and his gun came to hand as the knife rose. He fired, the lead tearing into Roscoe's guts at point-blank range.

Roscoe folded. The knife shuddered to a halt on its upward journey, then fell from his grasp. A second blast threw him on his back.

Mike stood over Roscoe, his gun aimed down at him as he ensured that this man would never return to the Cauldron to bushwhack Lucy. But when Roscoe's head lolled back and he stilled, Mike holstered his gun, then turned and headed to his horse.

He heard shouting and a growing commotion behind him, but he didn't look back, giving none of Last Hope's townsfolk any additional clues as to his identity.

But as nobody pursued him out of town he guessed that none of them cared too much about Roscoe's demise. Within a few miles he settled down to a steadier journey to Green Springs.

At a high point he halted his horse and looked back towards the Cauldron.

He couldn't see the plains or Entoro but somewhere out there was Lucy, a woman whom, if he didn't kill Galen quickly, he might never see again, but who was now safe from harm.

★ ★ ★

A day after Mike left Last Hope he rode into Green Springs.

He asked about Lazarus Heath and learnt that Roscoe was right — he had been recruiting men to ensure that he could take a consignment of gold from the Bone Gulch mine to Green Springs.

And when Mike asked where he might find him he was directed to the Silver Star saloon on the edge of town.

Mike entered the saloon and received

directions to a corner table, but when he stood before the table, he faced a solitary man.

And that man was Patrick Hancock.

With two whiskeys ordered, Mike considered Patrick.

'Not that it's any of my business,' he said, 'but why have you joined up with Lazarus Heath?'

Patrick fingered his glass.

'It was like you said to me back at Entoro: I needed to find out what I wanted to do, and joining Heath's outfit sounded a good idea.' Patrick leaned towards Mike. 'And that way I could earn me a living and get a chance to kill Galen.'

Mike snorted, fighting down his annoyance at this revelation.

'Because he's hiding in the Cauldron to pick off the miners?'

'You got it.' Patrick paused with his drink touching his lips. He lowered it, then raised his eyebrows. 'And you can join us. I reckon Lazarus is still hiring.'

'I work alone.'

Patrick raised a hand, smiling. 'When will you stop distrusting everyone, Mike? People want to help you, but you ain't interested.'

Mike slammed his glass on the table, spouting whiskey into the air.

'Because I'll get Galen myself. I don't need no help from anyone.'

'And what will happen when you catch up with him on your own? The last time you got a bullet in your guts and a broken leg.'

'I don't care about him killing me, just that I kill him,' Mike grunted, providing his traditional answer, but finding that this time the words sounded hollow and unconvincing. He glared hard at Patrick. 'Just tell me what you know about Galen and I'll do the rest.'

Patrick sighed. 'I don't understand you, Mike. You say you want to kill Galen, but you ain't going about it in a sensible way.'

Mike slammed his fist on the table, ready to grunt his irritation, but he stopped with the fist just above the table and despite his reluctance, he had to admit the sense in Patrick's suggestion.

'All right,' he murmured. 'Where do I find this Mr Heath?'

★　★　★

From under a lowered hat Lazarus Heath appraised Mike. His gaze was resolute as he appeared to be deciding whether to employ Mike purely from looking at him.

Standing beside Mike in the office at the side of the bank, Patrick was rocking from foot to foot.

'So,' Lazarus said, 'you want to join me, do you?'

Mike smiled. 'Yep.'

Lazarus's mouth twitched with a smile that, from the firmness of his jaw, Mike guessed was a rare occurrence.

'I'm looking for a special type of man.'

'And he is,' Patrick shouted, then slapped Mike's shoulder. 'He's already looked out for me and that just has to — '

'Patrick,' Lazarus murmured, while keeping his gaze on Mike, 'I'd be obliged if you'd let Mike speak for himself.'

'But, Lazarus, he — '

'And,' Lazarus snapped, turning to Patrick, 'I'd be obliged if you'd call me Mr Heath.'

'I'm sorry, Mr Heath,' Patrick murmured, then removed his hat to ruffle it before him. 'But I'm just saying that Mike is the kind of man we're looking for.'

'I am looking for,' Lazarus whispered. He rested his brow on his hand and, with his gaze set down, pointed at the door. 'Wait outside while I talk to Mike.'

Patrick's mouth fell open with shock, but he closed it, then patted Mike's back and scampered outside.

'He's still enthusiastic,' Mike said when the door slammed shut.

'That's one word for him.' Lazarus

sighed and raised his head. 'Have you formed a friendship with him?'

'I only got to know him by accident. He's too young and eager for my liking. But I ain't holding that against him, yet.'

Lazarus shrugged. 'Patrick might be useful, but without guidance, maybe not.'

'If that's your way of asking whether I'll look out for him, that ain't what I'm signing up for.'

'I understand. He either curbs his enthusiasm or he'll end up dead.' Lazarus narrowed his eyes. 'But if you don't want to look out for Patrick, what do you want?'

Mike fixed Lazarus with a firm gaze.

'I want to work. You want to hire someone. I can do the work. It ain't more complicated than that.'

'But the work will be dangerous. I intend to take out a major consignment of gold from Bone Gulch and that's sure to entice Galen Benitez. And whether it does or not, I will find him and eliminate him. Does that sound like work you can do?'

Mike fought down a sudden desire to shout his enthusiasm for this mission.

'Yeah,' he grunted through clenched teeth.

Lazarus stared long and hard at Mike, then thrust out a hand.

'Then you're hired.'

Two hours later, Lazarus Heath congregated his men outside the bank.

He had twelve men in all, flanking a wagon. Several presented shiny grime-encrusted faces that suggested they were also miners. The rest had the cold-eyed looks of men hired to fight.

Patrick hailed Mike, then beckoned him to join the group. So Mike drew his horse to a halt beside the wagon and tipped his hat.

Most of his new colleagues stared at him with indifference. Several nudged their hats, but this lack of enthusiasm didn't stop Patrick from embarking on a round of introductions.

Even when Mike flashed Patrick a glare, he still continued introducing each man, only quietening when he came to the driver of the wagon: Tyrone McColl.

9

Mike considered Tyrone. Oddly, seeing him didn't surprise Mike as much as Patrick's nervous glances at him suggested it should. Mike reckoned that Tyrone wouldn't give up on Lucy easily, and he'd probably sought out work that would take him in and out of the Cauldron to keep his options open.

Tyrone looked at Mike, his narrowed eyes suggesting an accusation and a silent question, but he did nod.

And, with that being the extent of the exchange Mike wanted to have with him right now, he faced the edge of town and waited for Lazarus to give the order to move on out.

Presently, at a steady pace, Lazarus Heath's men headed out of Green Springs and towards the Cauldron.

But, to Mike's irritation, their route would take them through Last Hope on the way to the goldmine at Bone Gulch.

When he discovered this Mike was tempted to leave the group immediately, but having let Patrick persuade him to join them, he accepted that staying with this large group would give him the best chance of finding Galen.

He listened whenever anyone talked about Last Hope. Nobody mentioned Roscoe Woods's death, but he learned that the area was under the jurisdiction of Sheriff Beltran and that he had a law office in Last Hope. But the mention of his name induced so much grunting and spitting from Lazarus that Mike decided not to enquire into the history he had had with him.

For the journey Mike's colleagues carried out their duties with quiet efficiency, leaving just the enthusiastic Patrick to talk about every animal and bird he saw, every landmark he passed and anything that crossed his mind. Nobody made the mistake of talking to Patrick, and Mike soon found that he could tune out his prattle.

After a day spent with his new colleagues, Mike settled into their quiet way of working. He could tell that many in the group had worked together before and, as they functioned efficiently, they saw no reason to explain their duties to a newcomer.

But as they could work just as well without him Mike didn't volunteer for anything and stayed on the periphery of the group, although this did bring him into frequent contact with the talkative Patrick, who was also treated with the same benign disdain with which everyone treated Mike.

But when they made camp for the night, chatter and a relaxed atmosphere pervaded the group.

The most boisterous member, Brock Kline, regaled everyone with an outlandish tale from his past, in which whiskey, women and fighting — his only interests in life — featured prominently. And when everyone tired of the tale, the eldest member, Compton Murdock, dragged out a harmonica and played a jaunty tune.

Aside from Patrick, nobody went so far as to burst into song or to dance, but from the foot-tapping, Mike judged that everybody enjoyed the entertainment — aside from Tyrone, who sat outside the circle of men, eyeing everyone from under a lowered hat.

Later, when Tyrone volunteered to the first watch, Mike also volunteered and the two men headed to an elevated position away from the camp.

When Tyrone reached his position Mike broke the silence.

'Surprised you're still around,' he said.

Tyrone considered Mike.

'Had to do something.'

'I guess.' Mike stood in silence, waiting for the inevitable question, but it was a long time coming.

'Lucy turn you down, too, then?'

Mike had rehearsed his answer to this question, but now found that he didn't want to risk the distraction of making an enemy of Tyrone while he was close to completing his mission of killing Galen, and he bit it back.

'Seems you still don't understand the situation back at Entoro.'

Tyrone snorted. 'So, you left her on her own?'

'I did, but she's safe.'

'There's a whole heap of dangers out here.'

'I know, but she's safe.' Mike fixed Tyrone with a quiet stare, suggesting but not saying that he had a reason to know that this was true.

'I'd have never left her out here.'

'But you did.'

'Only because of you.'

Mike winced at the inevitable direction this conversation was taking.

'I'm not lying to you. I have feelings for her, but killing Galen is more important to me.'

Tyrone's eyes flared as he waved a fist at Mike.

'I knew it,' he muttered. 'I knew it.'

Mike took a deep breath, then made his offer not because he meant it but to smooth over this awkward meeting.

'You're right, but remember this: I have an aim in life. You don't.' He left the rest of this sentiment unsaid, hoping that Tyrone would understand that he was offering to step aside if Tyrone could prove to Lucy that he was the better man, but Tyrone stabbed a firm finger against his chest.

'You saying I ain't got nothing to offer her?'

Mike looked down at the finger, then shook his head, deciding that anything he said to Tyrone would only annoy him even more.

'I wasn't.' He turned his back and paced away to take up his position.

'Don't turn your back on me when I'm talking to you.'

Mike stopped and stood a moment, then carried on.

He exchanged no further conversation with Tyrone when they finished their watch, and each man avoided the other the next morning when they prepared to move out.

They were still avoiding each other when, in late morning, they rode into Last Hope.

As when Mike had ridden into the town before, faces peered out of doorways at them. His previous visit had been brief and nobody in town should suspect that Roscoe Woods's killer would return so quickly, so Mike kept his back straight, ensuring he appeared as confident as the others did.

When they pulled up Lazarus dispatched Compton Murdock to the store with a list of provision requirements while his men headed into the adjoining saloon.

Beside the door there was a poster. Mike stopped to read it. He discovered that it was a notice about the murder of Roscoe Woods. But the suspect was unnamed and had a description that was general enough to not cause Mike a problem — provided he didn't draw attention to himself.

Mike pulled back the cloth door-flap and entered the saloon. Inside, Heath's men had congregated at one end of the bar, a plank of rough-hewn wood atop a row of barrels. The other customers glared at them with sneers etched into their faces.

Patrick beckoned Mike over and Mike leaned against the bar beside him. He even replied to some of Patrick's prattle.

But before the bartender had delivered beers to everyone a new man paced through the saloon doorway. Behind him three other men lined up.

Each man glared at the line of Heath's men with their upper lips curled in distaste. The lead man spat on the floor.

'Trouble?' Mike murmured to Patrick.

'Yeah,' Patrick whispered from the corner of his mouth, then placed his glass on the bar behind him. 'That's Sheriff Beltran.'

'Now look who's here,' Beltran said, folding his substantial arms and running his surly gaze along the row of men at the bar. 'Loser Heath is in town.'

Lazarus Heath turned and looked Beltran up and down, then snorted.

'And,' he said, 'Sheriff Useless is hiding in the saloon *again*. But what do you expect when Galen Benitez is about?'

Beltran shrugged. 'Galen can't kill a lawman.'

Lazarus pushed himself from the bar and stood with his legs planted wide.

'You ain't indestructible, even when you hide under your bed like a scared child.' Lazarus flared his eyes and chuckled.

'You're wrong. If he kills me, another man with integrity will pin on a star and get him.'

'Galen won't get the chance. I've hired a whole heap of dependable men to do your job for you.'

His men grunted their approval.

'And if your miners didn't head here and shoot up the place so often, I could spare the time to catch Galen.' Knowing nods and grunts rippled around the saloon as Beltran paced round on the spot, sporting a lively grin, then stopped and aped Lazarus's posture with his feet wide and his hands on his hips. 'But I guess when Galen's killed you, my problems will be over. There'll be no big snakes left to crawl out of the Cauldron.'

Lazarus sneered and turned his back on Beltran, but as Beltran peeled out a roar of laughter and slapped his thigh, Brock Kline pushed himself from the bar and stood beside Lazarus.

'You insult Lazarus Heath,' he shouted, clenching his fists, 'you insult us all. So, take that back.'

Beltran slapped his thigh one last time, then let his laughter ripple into silence.

'And if I don't?'

Brock took a long and belligerent pace towards Beltran.

'I'll pound your head into the ground and keep on pounding until you do take it back.'

Beltran sneered. 'Lay one finger on a lawman and you won't get out of a cell until long after Galen has killed every last one of you.'

As Brock rolled his shoulders and glanced at his large fist, Mike pushed himself from the bar and joined Brock. Mike judged that this confrontation was threatening to put them all in a cell, so he slapped a firm hand on Brock's shoulder and whispered calming words.

Brock's jaw muscles rippled and his fists opened and closed, but he stayed rooted to the spot.

Beltran glared hard at Brock, then at the rest of Heath's men. He snorted and turned to leave the saloon. His three colleagues lined up to spit on the floor before Brock's boots, then turn and follow him out.

In response, Brock snorted his breath through his nostrils, but Mike dug his fingers into Brock's shoulder.

'Ignore them,' he said. 'Your beer's getting warm.'

Brock shrugged Mike's hand away and when the last man bent to spit on the floor, he darted his foot forward so that the spit splattered his grime-encrusted boot.

'Hey,' Brock muttered, 'you dirtied my boot.'

The last man sneered and paced up to stand before Brock. With a sly grin on his face, he rolled his tongue around his mouth and spat a huge gob of spit on Brock's other boot.

'Now they're both cleaner,' he said.

Brock's face reddened, his fists opening and closing.

'Brock,' Mike urged, 'you can't hit a lawman, no matter what he does.'

The man shrugged. 'But I ain't no lawman. Beltran only has two deputies. I just help out.'

Brock's eyes gleamed. 'I'd hoped you'd say that.'

Brock hurled himself at the man and, even as his blow to the jaw was sending him skidding across the floor, everyone else in the saloon scraped back their chairs.

Almost without Mike realizing what was happening, everybody in the saloon had squared off to a member of Heath's men and numerous individual fights had started.

Mike now accepted he'd never get out of town without a full-scale fight erupting, so he swung round and weighed into the nearest man, flailing his fists.

He hurled a flurry of blows at the man's face, several connecting and knocking his head one way, then the other. Then he grabbed his shoulders, turned him round, and ran him at a table. He released his hold as they reached the table and the momentum hurled the man over it and bundled him into the wall of the tent.

Mike stood a moment, rolling his shoulders, then glanced around, looking for his next assailant.

Each of his comrades had at least one opponent and some were taking on two. Even so, everyone was keeping an eye on Lazarus and Sheriff Beltran, who had moved into the centre of the saloon and were circling each other with their fists raised.

Then a hand slapped on Mike's shoulder and swung him round.

The man he faced had the bleary-eyed look of the heavily drunk, but he had his fists raised high. This man hurled back a fist, but then lowered it and narrowed his eyes.

'Wait a moment,' the man grunted. 'I recognize you.'

10

Mike's guts turned to ice as he recognized his opponent as being the man who had directed him to Roscoe Woods in this very saloon.

He side-stepped the man and grabbed a glass of beer from the bar, then took a swig, using the distraction to consider his predicament. He decided that knocking this man unconscious would resolve his problem in the short term, but that it might also help to convince him that Mike really was the man who killed Roscoe Woods.

'You must be mistaken.' He raised the glass and smiled. 'I'm just enjoying my drink.'

The man rolled his shoulders, the action lurching him back a pace.

'No, I know you from somewhere.' He righted himself and kneaded his forehead. 'Can't remember where.'

As the man peered at him with one eye closed, Mike glanced at the nearest fighting twosome, then darted his head back as a thrown chair hurtled by his nose and crashed into the bar.

'Sorry, friend. You got the wrong man. I'm just passing through.' Mike tipped his hat. 'And now I'm leaving.'

As the man clapped his mouth soundlessly Mike turned and, with his hat pulled low, snaked his way outside, giving the fighters a wide berth. Outside, he wandered down the road to the wagon where Compton had moved the provisions he'd just bought to the edge of town.

Compton glanced up as Mike approached, then returned to staring at the heaps of provisions and then down at the list he still clutched.

From the corner of his eye Mike confirmed that the man hadn't followed him out, but when he joined Compton he searched for something to say to make it appear that he was unconcerned.

'You get a good price?' he asked.

Compton glanced at Mike, then shrugged and returned his gaze to the provisions.

'We struck an adequate bargain,' he murmured. 'Although I reckon that storekeeper has taken advantage of me. That bag doesn't look like ten pounds of coffee.'

'Then take it back. I'll guard the provisions.'

Compton nodded and, as he headed back to the store with the lightweight bag, Mike sat on the back of the wagon. He watched Compton disappear from view, but then a huge crash sounded in the saloon, followed by Brock Kline tumbling through the door, backwards.

But Brock shook his head, jumped to his feet, and charged back into the saloon.

As the man who'd recognized him still hadn't appeared, Mike sat back and listened to the sounds emerging from the saloon, of glass smashing, raised voices, and furniture crashing to the floor.

But within five minutes quiet descended on the saloon.

Sheriff Beltran and his deputies emerged first. They had Brock held between them.

Lazarus hurried out of the saloon and, with his men flanking him, gesticulated and grunted at Beltran.

From one hundred yards away Mike couldn't hear the argument, but he guessed that Heath's men had tried to avoid hitting the lawmen in the saloon. But Brock had shown no such restraint and had now been arrested, that incident ending the fight.

Lazarus and Beltran traded another round of insults but, with a contemptuous wave, Beltran ordered his deputies to release Brock. They threw him to the ground, then swaggered away.

Brock leapt to his feet and hurried after them, shouting taunts and kicking dirt at their backs, but Lazarus ordered him to desist. Brock ignored him and continued shouting, but Lazarus grabbed Brock's shoulders and dragged him back. By degrees Brock calmed and the troop of men turned and headed back to the wagon.

With each pace the walking turned to swaggering and the men exchanged a round of backslapping as they swapped boasts about how many of the saloon's customers they had each defeated.

Patrick was limping but he still managed to grin and even Tyrone was rolling his shoulders and laughing.

Then Brock saw Mike sitting on the back of the wagon and, with a slap in the stomach to the two men flanking him, he forced everyone to halt.

Brock strode forward a pace.

'Mike,' he grunted, 'what you doing out here?'

'Guarding the wagon,' Mike said, jumping to the ground. 'Don't want anybody stealing our provisions.'

'That ain't it,' Tyrone announced, pacing up to stand beside Brock, a gleam appearing in his eyes. 'Mike took one look at the fight then ran like a yellow-bellied skunk.'

As Brock, then the other men, murmured support, Mike glared hard at Tyrone, seeing a surprising amount of conviction in his firm gaze.

'You got it wrong.'

Tyrone set his feet wide and rolled his shoulders.

'Prove it.'

'Yeah,' Brock said, grinning. 'Prove it.'

Mike looked at Brock, then at Tyrone while he searched for a way to end this argument quickly so that they could leave town before the man who had recognized him emerged from the saloon. He had just decided that hitting Tyrone would probably be the quickest way when Lazarus slapped Tyrone's shoulder and pointed at the wagon.

'We haven't got time for this,' he said. 'We're heading out.'

'I ain't heading out with someone I don't trust, Mr Heath,' Tyrone said, receiving grunted support from Brock.

'Tyrone, Brock, you've had enough fighting for one day. Save your spirit for seeing off Galen.'

Brock nodded and headed to his horse, but Tyrone continued to glare at Mike. Then he shrugged and backed towards the wagon, but a knowing smile appeared as he climbed into the seat and raised the reins.

With the evaporation of the confrontation, everyone made ready to leave town. Within five minutes they headed out of Last Hope.

Even so, Mike reckoned that he was being watched. So, at a bend in the trail where the town disappeared from view, he glanced back.

To his relief, in Last Hope nobody was outside and looking his way, but Tyrone was glaring at him. Mike sneered and faced the front, but Tyrone's insistent gaze still warmed the back of his neck.

★ ★ ★

Although Heath's men had travelled in silence on the way to Last Hope, aside from Patrick's chatter, for the rest of the day the fight in the saloon caused the situation to be reversed.

Patrick lapsed into quietness but everyone else discussed the fight. As the sun edged towards the horizon the boasts became more outlandish and the number of people they'd defeated grew.

And whenever everyone had exhausted their tales, Tyrone whipped up the enthusiasm by restarting the discussion with another wild boast.

Lazarus didn't stop the banter and Tyrone didn't offer any more comments about Mike's lack of involvement in the fight, but the failure to hear his name uttered provided a more effective taunt than anything else could.

At sundown they made camp.

Nobody would come close to him or meet his eye and, with even the normally talkative Patrick avoiding him, Mike volunteered to take the first watch. And when he returned Tyrone had thankfully run out of new boasts about the fight in Last Hope.

Even so Tyrone repeatedly looked at him and licked his lips. His eager grin suggested he was searching for more ways to use the situation in Last Hope to further browbeat the man he now believed to be his rival for Lucy's affections.

But Mike said nothing and gave him no opportunity to strengthen his advantage. So, with everyone pointedly avoiding him, he spent a quiet night.

In the morning Mike made his ritual promise that Galen would be dead by sundown, but the same level of ignoring continued as he ate then prepared to move out.

And when Mike headed to his horse he saw that someone had found a yellow flower and placed it on his saddle, then spelt out 'yeller' in stones beside the saddle.

'Anything wrong?' Tyrone shouted, jumping to his feet and grinning.

'Nope.' Mike kicked the flower away, then rocked back his foot to scuff the stones away.

'That must mean you're yellow like the stones say.'

Mike lowered his foot and turned to face Tyrone.

'So, you wrote that, did you?'

Tyrone set his hands on his hips. 'Sure did.'

'Figures. The fact you can't spell explains plenty.'

A couple of other men snickered, causing Tyrone to redden.

'You calling me something, yellow-belly?'

'I ain't no yellow-belly and I ain't saying nothing about you that ain't true.'

Tyrone rolled his shoulders and advanced a long pace on Mike, but Lazarus paced into the middle of them and raised his hands.

'That's enough,' he shouted, looking left and right at each man in turn. 'We got a long journey ahead and we got to keep on the look-out for Galen Benitez. So, stop bickering and move out.'

With much grumbling Tyrone slouched away and the group did move out.

But with Patrick remaining in his sullen mood and refusing to catch his eye Mike suffered the quietest day of his journey to Bone Gulch so far. And Tyrone frequently glanced at him and smiled as he enjoyed Mike's predicament.

That night they camped on the edge of the plains, close to the spot where Mike had first met Lucy. The location was easily defendable as it provided a clear view of anyone approaching from the hills behind them or from across the plains.

Still, Lazarus posted men on both approaches with orders for changes in look-outs every two hours.

But they spent another quiet night and, with Mike avoiding Tyrone and giving him no opportunity to refuel their disagreement, Tyrone ran out of confrontational comments to direct at Mike. As he retired for the night and made his ritual promise, Mike even hoped that the distraction of this argument would peter out the next day.

An hour after first light Heath's men headed across the plains towards Bone Gulch.

Later in the morning they edged closer to Snake Ridge and Mike looked towards Entoro where Lucy was detailing the patterns on the boulders and mapping the area. He bit back a pang of sorrow that he couldn't see her from such a distance. And he wondered what she would think if she were able to see the group heading past.

But when he noticed that Tyrone was also looking towards Entoro he looked to the sky and located the faint shape of the young crescent moon. He judged that he had around ten days before the full moon, which ought to be enough time to reach Bone Gulch, kill Galen, and return before Lucy left, but only if he was lucky and Galen raided them.

When he turned to face the front he saw that Tyrone was glaring at him. His wide eyes suggested that he'd seen Mike looking towards Entoro and that he was now even more determined to provoke a fight with Mike and to strengthen everyone's distrust of him.

And sure enough, that night, with dinner served, Tyrone loomed over him.

'What's wrong, Mike?' he muttered with laughter in his tone. 'Is the meat too brown for you? Perhaps you'd prefer *yellow* meat?'

Mike winced at the inevitability of Tyrone's taunts.

'I wouldn't.' Mike tapped his plate. 'This is just fine.'

'Just fine? Then perhaps you don't understand what I'm saying.' Tyrone slammed his hands on his hips and bent at the waist to thrust his face into Mike's face. 'I say you have a yellow streak.'

'You know that's wrong.' Mike speared a lump of meat and gulped it down. 'And now, I'll finish my meal.'

Tyrone shrugged and backed, but he returned with a handful of stones. He placed them on the ground before Mike to spell out 'Y' then continued until he'd finished his word. This time he spelt it right.

'See, I can learn,' Tyrone said, standing back. 'I ain't good with lettering, but once someone tells me what I've done wrong, I get it right next time. But that's your problem, Mike. You're yellow and you'll never change.' Tyrone chuckled. 'Unless you want to make me change my mind.'

Mike considered his next lump of meat, then threw down his plate and rolled to his feet.

'You ain't got a mind to change.'

'Good,' Tyrone muttered. He spat on his right fist. 'I've been waiting for you to show some fire.'

Mike ignored the fist and stared into Tyrone's eyes.

'You know I have fire. And I'll tear your head off if you push me, but I'm trying to save that fire for the right moment.' Mike flexed his fists. 'But if you're determined to get by without a head, say I'm yellow again.'

Tyrone slapped his chest, grinning. 'You're yell — '

Mike burst into a run, thrusting his

head down, and ploughed into Tyrone before he could finish his word.

The air blasted out of Tyrone's chest as Mike knocked him back for five paces until Tyrone's right leg slipped and he tumbled on his back, dragging Mike with him.

But as they hit the ground, Tyrone pushed his legs up, wheeling Mike over his head.

Mike somersaulted before landing flat on his back, but he rolled to the side then jumped to his feet. He swirled round and walked into a pile-driving blow to the chin that snapped his head back and a flurry of blows to the chest that made his sore ribs protest.

But Mike danced back to move out of Tyrone's range while he regained his breath.

Tyrone stared at him, grinning. Misplaced confidence burned in his intent gaze as everyone shouted encouragement at him to beat Mike to a pulp.

When he moved in Mike urged him

on by clutching his ribs and wincing. But when Tyrone swung his first punch, Mike swayed back from it and, while Tyrone was off balance, scythed a round-armed blow to his cheek that rocked his head down. And an uppercut to his chin snapped him back on his heels.

Then Mike pressed home his advantage, delivering punches fast and hard that pummelled Tyrone's chest and face, finishing off with a haymaker of a slug to his chin that swung him round. A kick to the rump ploughed him into the dirt.

Tyrone lay for a moment, then rolled on to his back and sat up. His shoulders hunched and his eyes glazed as his fighting spirit appeared to leave him.

Still Mike stood over him, his fists raised; then he glanced around, ensuring that everyone saw that he'd won the fight fairly and that he'd settled their argument.

Brock was the first to nod and a series of grunts went up from the others as everyone noted that Tyrone's taunts about Mike's unwillingness to fight were unjustified.

Mike looked down at Tyrone and offered his hand in the hope that Tyrone would accept that the better man had won, but Tyrone snorted then darted his hand into his jacket. Metal flashed.

Mike scrambled for his gun, the weapon clearing leather in a smooth motion, but as he raised it, a gun blast echoed, the slug tearing the gun from Mike's hand.

'Mike!' Lazarus snapped as he paced towards them, his gun raised. 'That's enough.'

'He was going to shoot me,' Mike said. He flexed his fingers, as Tyrone withdrew his hand from his jacket and the glint of metal disappeared.

Lazarus shook his head. 'The only man I saw with a gun was you.'

Tyrone snorted his agreement and even held his hands high, palms up, showing that he didn't hold a weapon.

A chorus of comments went up from the others, and they all supported him.

Mike snorted. 'You all got that wrong. He was going for a weapon.'

Lazarus stood before Mike and sneered.

'I spoke up for you earlier to keep peace in the camp and because I reckoned you had a good reason for avoiding that fight in Last Hope. Now, I'm wondering if I was mistaken.'

Lazarus raised his eyebrows, inviting a response.

Mike glanced around, seeing no possibility of support in everyone's surly gazes. Even Patrick wouldn't meet his gaze and Tyrone was biting his bottom lip to suppress a grin after the unexpected extent of his success.

'Somebody had to protect the provisions in Last Hope and I took that on myself.'

He glanced at Compton, but received a sneer.

'I was already outside,' Compton said, 'when Mike left the saloon.'

Lazarus nodded then glared at Mike, possibly hoping he'd provide another feeble excuse, but when Mike stayed quiet, he snorted.

'New men are usually eager to please. But you ain't and that means you don't plan to stay with us for long. And even if you've just proved you ain't the kind of man who would walk away from a fight, I don't reckon you wanted to defend our provisions.'

'What you getting at?'

Lazarus paced in a circle before turning to face Mike.

'I don't like Sheriff Beltran, but I worry when a man avoids a lawman.'

'I didn't,' Mike said, trying to force sincerity into his voice as he fixed Lazarus with his firm gaze.

'Maybe you did or maybe you didn't, but I reckon you're trouble I just don't need.'

Lazarus returned Mike's gaze, but then flicked it up over Mike's shoulder.

Mike just had time to tense, but then firm footfalls stomped behind him.

Hands grabbed him from behind and yanked his arms up his back. Mike struggled, trying to throw the men away, but found that they'd gained a firm grasp of him and he had no choice but to let them hold him.

'You got it all wrong,' he shouted. 'Search Tyrone's jacket before you do anything.'

Lazarus flicked his gaze to the side, providing a silent gesture to someone out of Mike's sight and Mike heard another man close in on him, the paces slow and deliberate.

'Be quiet,' Lazarus said. 'Out here I don't have no law to tell me what to do, so I make my own justice. And you're about to find out how I do that.'

11

'You got no right doing this!' Mike screeched.

Lazarus stood over him, the early-morning sun casting his shadow over Mike's supine form.

'You broke every one of my rules,' Lazarus said. 'So, I got every right to deal with you in any way I see fit.'

Mike struggled against his bonds, but still found them as secure as ever. He had spent a long, sleepless night staked out on the ground, his arms and legs splayed, the stakes driven deep into the unforgiving ground.

His only comfort had been the possibility that a night spent in this painful position was the extent of the punishment that Lazarus had decided to inflict on him. But now that everyone was ready to move out, the terrible fear that Lazarus really did intend to leave him here to rot was threatening to overcome him.

'You got me wrong,' Mike said, keeping his voice level and his gaze firm. 'Trust me.'

'But I don't, and I can't take a man with me that I don't trust.'

'I had no reason to avoid no lawman or avoid no fight or shoot Tyrone without provocation.'

'And perhaps you're right. So, when we return, I'll take you to Last Hope and let you explain yourself to Sheriff Beltran.' Lazarus laughed. 'Provided the buzzards have left anything for us to find.'

Mike saw no chance of a reprieve in Lazarus's cold gaze. He glanced up at the other men, seeking out Patrick, who provided a shocked glance but then turned away.

None of the other men returned his gaze, although Brock and Compton did shoot glances at him, then shake their heads, suggesting that they didn't agree with Lazarus's punishment, but saw no reason to stop him.

Then everyone left Mike's sight.

Mike lay, looking up at the sky, the low sun to his side, listening to the troop of men bustle, then move out, still hoping that maybe Lazarus would reprieve him at the last moment. But the hoofbeats receded.

Then, just as the terrible certainty of his fate was overcoming Mike, he heard wheels trundle closer.

He darted his gaze to the side, but then saw that Tyrone had taken the wagon on a circuit around him. Tyrone leaned forward in the seat, grinning, then looked over his shoulder towards the direction of Entoro, but as he turned back, Mike looked the other way, refusing to let him enjoy whatever taunts he'd planned.

But Tyrone said nothing and presently, he hurried the wagon on, leaving Mike.

And then he was alone.

Without much hope, Mike began systematically tugging on the ropes that pinned his limbs to the ground. He alternated between his right and left arm and, using his small amount of leverage, tugged his wrists as far as he could, but no matter how hard he pulled, the stakes remained firm.

He had been lucky in that Lazarus hadn't added any cruel twists to his fate such as soaking the ropes so that they'd tighten in the heat of the day. So, Mike fortified himself with the thought that maybe this meant he did intend to return for him and then hand him in to Sheriff Beltran.

But that possibility was several days away and he didn't hold out much hope that he would still be alive to see his reprieve. So, while he still had the strength, he continued to tug on his ropes and frantically riffle through his mind for a plan that might drag him out of this hopeless predicament.

Fortunately, Lazarus had staked him out on a slight slope and, by straining his neck to the side, he could see along the extent of Snake Ridge and even see the slight undulation that marked the location of Entoro. He resolved that when his strength left him, he would ensure his head rolled that way so that he could die looking towards Lucy.

And that time came sooner than he feared.

The sun rose until it was high above him and baked fearsome heat down on him, blasting all moisture from his body far more quickly than on his last journey across the Cauldron without water. At least then he had rested in the shade, but here he could do nothing but look up and let the sun slowly bake him to death.

Buzzards circled overhead, their routes trailing down closer and closer, some even disappearing as they ventured on to the ground, then began squabbling over their forthcoming feast.

Such was his desperate state that he even welcomed them, judging that, like his earlier finding of the stage, they might attract a rare traveller to him.

But even that hope couldn't console him and he thrust his head to the side to look towards Entoro.

A shadow fell across him, providing temporary relief from the sun, but Mike knew that it had to be an emboldened buzzard. He flinched and uttered the loudest screech he could muster. But the shadow didn't move.

Mike dragged in his breath to screech again when the shadow lengthened over him and he saw that it was a man's shadow. Mike snapped his head back, looking behind him and breathed in a grating sigh when he saw that Patrick had returned.

'Patrick,' he breathed, 'you've come for me. Get these bonds off me will you?'

Patrick paced round to stand beside him. He looked the bonds over, then looked Mike in the eye.

'Why should I?'

Mike blinked back his surprise.

'You came back for me, didn't you?'

'I did, but I had to find out.' He hunkered down beside him and fingered a rope. 'I thought you were the strongest, most resourceful man I'd ever met, but then you walked away from a fight. Tyrone says you did it because you're yellow and Lazarus reckons you did it to avoid Sheriff Beltran. I don't know what the answer is, so I've come back to hear it.'

'And if I tell you and you don't like my answer, will you just leave me here?'

Patrick flicked another rope.

'I don't know if I could do that, but like you said, I did come back for you, so tell me the truth.'

Mike nudged his head back, signifying the plains behind him.

'How did you get away?'

'I rode at the back with your horse in tow and fell further and further back. Nobody urged me on, so I just hid the first chance I got, then came back. But stop changing the subject and tell me.'

Mike breathed a sigh of relief, judging that if Patrick had brought two horses with him, he probably wouldn't leave him here.

'Just trust me. Release me and I'll tell you everything.'

'No!' Patrick slapped the rope holding Mike's right arm. 'Tell me everything now!'

Mike rasped a dry tongue over his parched lips as he weighed up the numerous lies he could tell Patrick that would ensure he got free, but then shrugged.

'I walked out on the fight in Last Hope to avoid drawing attention to myself.' He looked into Patrick's eyes. 'I killed Roscoe Woods in the town earlier.'

Patrick blinked hard. 'I don't believe that.'

Mike uttered a harsh laugh. 'I tell you the truth and you don't believe it. But I did, and as you know Lucy, and, I think, care about her, you should know that I had to. Roscoe killed Holman Reynolds. He took him in the Cauldron and slit his throat. And as I reckoned he'd do the same to Lucy, I had to kill him.'

'You should have got Sheriff Beltran to deal with him.'

'Perhaps I should, but I had no proof and I've got used to dealing with trouble my own way.' Mike smiled. 'So, now you've heard the truth, what are you going to do?'

Ten minutes later, Mike sat on a rock beside Patrick, alternating between rubbing his scraped wrists and gulping water.

'I hope I did the right thing,' Patrick said.

'You sure did,' Mike croaked. He slapped Patrick's arm, then jumped down from the rock. 'And now, I got to go.'

'You going after Galen, or Lazarus, or Tyrone?'

'Galen is always first, but I guess I got scores to settle against the other two now.'

Patrick raised a finger.

'You're wrong. We have scores to settle.'

Mike considered Patrick a moment, then sighed.

'Yeah. We have scores to settle.'

164

★ ★ ★

Late in the day they passed the spot where Mike had tried his assault on Galen and afterwards they headed from the plains and reached the side of the precipitous mountain that contained Bone Gulch.

Mike used the last rays of the setting sun to peer up the trail ahead but saw no sign of Heath's men. Even so, they made camp and set off again at first light.

The route was a clear one, but the slope was fierce. When they reached the tree-line it was just wide enough to ride with a foot of clear space on either side.

Later in the morning Mike had the first hint that his quest might be close to completion when the intensity of the tracks on the trail increased. He backtracked and found that a separate trail wound away through the trees and that a new set of prints headed along it before joining the main trail.

'Is that Galen,' Patrick said, 'following after Lazarus?'

Mike shrugged. 'No way of knowing for sure, but it's a reasonable guess that Galen is on Lazarus's trail.'

Patrick provided a nervous smile.

'Then let's hope they all wipe each other out before we catch up with them.'

Mike would normally have grunted his disgust at this thought, but this time he nodded and slapped Patrick's arm.

'Let's hope for Galen's sake that you're right. With the likes of us behind him, he has no chance.'

He winked and received a smile in return. Then they resumed following the tracks.

Neither he nor Patrick knew for sure how far it was to Bone Gulch. But as the day wore on and they climbed higher, Mike assumed that it would be a long journey and that he'd get the first inkling that they were getting close when he heard gunfire ahead as Galen ambushed Lazarus.

But when he rounded a sharp bend, with Patrick several horse-lengths behind him, coming down the trail ahead was a line of riders.

12

Mike pulled back on the reins as he looked up the slope.

He saw that the riders who were heading towards him were Heath's men. Lazarus was riding up front beside a wagon. Tyrone was driving the wagon and, from the stacked crates on the back, Mike presumed they had already collected the gold from Bone Gulch and were now heading back to Green Springs.

Lazarus flinched back in his saddle, but then ripped out his gun while shouting orders to his men to capture Mike.

Mike swung his horse around, aiming to get back round the bend quickly, but then Lazarus blasted a volley of lead at him. His horse reared and he had to calm it before setting off.

But then a sickening thud sounded

and his horse reared again, shaking its head.

Mike registered that the noise he'd heard was lead tearing into flesh, then his horse's legs buckled and tipped him sideways. Mike saw the spray of blood bursting from his horse's neck and had no choice but to leap from the saddle.

He hit the trail and rolled, while his horse tumbled in the opposite direction and fell away from the trail and down the slope. But Mike came up on his feet and ran up the slope then into the trees.

He scrambled up the sharp slope, lead cannoning into the trees around him, but the trees were so thick that the trail behind him quickly disappeared from view and the gunfire petered out.

At a fallen tree he hunkered down and took stock of his situation. Patrick hadn't followed him around the bend and he hoped the young man had had the sense to take cover.

Down on the trail Lazarus was still shouting orders for his men to capture him.

Mike looked up the slope. He decided that he would quickly become lost if he carried on uphill, so he searched for the best cover in the branches of the fallen tree, hoping that Lazarus wouldn't waste much time searching for him.

Then he saw a flash of clothing through the trees. One of Heath's men hurried into view. That man flinched on seeing Mike, then swung behind a tree and shouted out that he'd found him.

Mike turned, but then felt and heard the whine of a bullet rip past his shoulder. He swirled round and saw that Lazarus had outflanked him and was now running diagonally down the slope towards him.

Lazarus fired again, the lead winging wide, then he slid to a halt and hunkered down.

Mike vaulted the tree and threw himself to the ground behind it. He drew his gun and fired at the tree that the other man was hiding behind, keeping that man pinned down, then he slammed the gun on the trunk of the tree and fired blind at Lazarus.

Then he risked glancing up. Lazarus was now running sideways to him, aiming to take cover behind a tree. Mike hurried him on his way with two quick shots, but on the second the man behind him fired, tearing splinters out of the wood beside Mike's hand.

Mike rolled the other way, swinging his gun round and tore a shot at the man which forced him to take cover, but ten yards to that man's right another man appeared, snaking between the trees.

Mike fired a speculative shot at him, then scrambled for bullets from his gun-belt. As he punched in the first slug both of the men jumped out from their cover. They laid down a sustained burst of gunfire at Mike, who had no choice but to jump to his feet and roll over the trunk to lie on the other side.

He stared up the slope. As he slammed in the last bullet Lazarus darted out from his covering tree and took careful aim at him. But as Mike swung his gun up, Lazarus staggered back, a red star bursting across his chest.

He righted himself, but another burst of redness exploded from his neck. He stood straight, then fell forward. With no control of his movements, he rolled down the slope until he slammed into the fallen tree.

Mike glanced around, judging that Patrick was hidden somewhere close and had saved him, but he rolled round and planted his gun on the tree, aiming down the slope.

'You men,' he shouted, 'my argument was with Lazarus, not with any of you. We've sorted that out now and, if you're still looking for help in defending your gold against Galen Benitez, I'm available.'

Mike heard mumbled comments from below and judged that they were, at least, considering his offer, and when he ventured a glance over the trunk, he saw nobody. He continued to stare and saw one man, but he was running with his back to him and was closing on the trail.

Then footfalls pattered as Patrick ran doubled-over towards him and skidded to a halt behind the tree.

'Seems as if they're leaving,' Patrick said, hunkering down at his side.

'They are, and I'm obliged,' Mike said, 'again.'

'No trouble, but did you mean what you said? Would you really join them again?'

'You forget — I only want to kill Galen.'

Patrick shrugged. 'Then remember this — we were following Galen's tracks and he was following Lazarus. So, where is Galen if we've met these men first?'

Mike winced, then glanced around. 'Somewhere close.'

He slapped Patrick's shoulder then hurried away to confirm that Lazarus was dead. Then they headed through the trees to where Patrick had left his horse.

Mike glanced out on to the trail, confirming that nobody was close, then edged along the trail and ventured a glance around the bend. He saw that further up the slope the men had bunched together, but Compton was standing before them and gesticulating while barking orders. Mike couldn't hear what he was saying, but within a minute the group turned and filed towards them. And Compton rode up front beside Tyrone.

'Compton looks like he's taken over,' Patrick said, peering over Mike's shoulder.

'Yeah, and I judge that he was a more reasonable man than Lazarus was. So, I reckon we should try to join them.'

'You still sure about this? Nobody was happy with Lazarus staking you out, but they didn't stop him.'

Mike glanced at Patrick's horse. 'Then put it this way — would you prefer us to ride doubled-up for the next few days.'

'All right, but let me do — '

A huge crack snapped out to the side, the noise deafening.

Mike swirled round to look at the trees further up the slope and saw what had caused the sound — a tree was falling over beside the trail, its future route arcing down towards the back of the group of men.

Frantically, everyone sped on down the trail to avoid the falling tree. It crashed to the ground, its outermost branches brushing past the rearmost rider.

As the group whooped their delight at having avoided the potential disaster, Mike hurried up the slope towards them. Behind him, Patrick swung on to his horse and followed.

But as soon as Tyrone saw Mike he snapped back in his seat, then glared down the slope at him. With a huge snap of his arms, he shook the reins and hurried his horse on, aiming for Mike and recklessly swaying the wagon closer to the edge of the trail in his haste to run him down.

In the middle of the thin trail Mike slid to a halt, but on seeing the wagon horses bearing down on him he threw himself to the side. He tumbled over the side of the trail then rolled to lie flat on his belly. Even so he slid ten feet before he could dig his feet into the ground and stop his sliding.

He looked up, seeing Tyrone hurtle by, his rival only having enough time to glare down at him before he passed from his view. Then Mike scrambled up the slope to reach the trail again.

But as he rolled back on top another huge creak sounded to one side and another tree toppled, heading down to land across the trail in front of the remainder of the men.

Compton and another man were below the falling tree and both men looked up, transfixed, but Compton was the first to break out of his spell. He dragged his horse back a pace.

Too late, the other man reacted, but by then the branches were ploughing into him and slamming him from his horse. Mike saw him disappear beneath a tangle of wood and instinctively knew that trying to get him out would be wasted effort.

To Mike's side, Patrick had pulled his horse off the trail to avoid Tyrone and the runaway wagon. Now he was hurrying after it.

But then Mike realized that the falling trees weren't their biggest problem.

It was windy, but not so windy that two trees should have fallen so close to each other.

Somebody had to have toppled those trees, and Mike knew who that person was.

'Galen Benitez,' he murmured to himself.

13

Mike shouted out a warning to Compton, but even as Compton was spinning round in the saddle the shooting started. It came from all directions, blasting down at them.

One man hurtled backwards from his horse, his chest pitted red, and Mike felt the whine of a bullet rip past his cheek.

Compton was shouting at everyone to dismount and regroup, but through the hail of bullets his orders were only adding to the chaos.

Down the trail Patrick had at last reached the wagon. Mike saw him swing on to the wagon seat.

But then Patrick stood upright and fell backwards. He hit the ground on his back, his taut posture as he fell suggesting he'd been shot.

As Tyrone leaned over the side of the

wagon to peer back at Patrick's body, Mike hurried to the tree. He scrambled through the branches and peered out, searching for the location of Galen's men.

But then a huge explosion ripped out behind him.

Dirt tore into Mike's back and hurled him forwards. As a wall of noise echoed in his ears, the force of the explosion rolled him out of the branches. Beside him a series of agonized cries went up.

He looked over his shoulder to see that the explosion had dislodged a fifty-foot length of the trail, and now the earth was tumbling inexorably downwards.

The men dragged their horses back, but at least two weren't fast enough and the rolling dirt swept them from the trail to disappear from view.

Brock was on Mike's side of the landslide and he was hurrying to get out of the way. Mike urged him on, but then Brock slipped to his knees and rolled.

On his other side Mike saw movement. Several of Galen's men were clambering down the mountainside and, in their midst, was Galen Benitez.

Mike hunkered down, sure that these men hadn't realized that he was so close, but then he saw a flash of clothing to his side and swirled round. He saw Brock wheel by, his arms flailing but unable to control his descent.

Mike looked left and right. He glanced at the tumbling Brock, then at the gold-wagon as it trundled around the bend, then at Galen.

For just a moment Galen looked at him. He cocked his head to one side, grinning, perhaps in acknowledgement that Mike had survived to face him. But then, without a moment's thought, Mike turned his back on Galen and lunged out from the branches. His fist clasped around Brock's waving arm and halted his movement.

Brock and he locked gazes.

'Grab my other arm,' Mike shouted.

Brock flared his eyes, then lunged, but as his fingers brushed Mike's sleeve another explosion tore out from the mountainside and a solid wall of earth ploughed into them. Mike grabbed a branch and, as he refused to release Brock's arm, his injured leg delivered a rare protesting bolt of pain, but then the force of the landslide tore the branch from his grasp.

Mike rolled forward into the dirt and tumbled after Brock down the slope. He had never experienced a situation where he couldn't trust the ground beneath his feet and he could do nothing but flounder and fight to keep his head from going under the dirt.

But then he slammed to a halt. He fought and shook himself, ensuring he stayed above ground, but then felt the arms that were wrapped around his shoulders and realized that Brock was dragging him on to a boulder.

He kicked at the earth, helping Brock pull him free. Then he lay beside him and looked around. The boulder was an island of calm in a sea of moving earth. Most of the mountainside appeared to be rumbling by, although he detected that it was calmer now that the first explosions had subsided. He turned to Brock.

'Obliged.'

'No problem for someone who tried to save me.' Brock took a deep breath, then slapped Mike's shoulder. 'And I got to admit you ain't no yellow-belly like Tyrone said. And I wish I'd spoken up for you when . . . '

Mike sighed as Brock looked away. He had chosen to save Brock rather than try to kill Galen, but he didn't know whether to feel anger or pleasure about his humane action. He looked up the slope, searching for Galen and gritting his teeth, but he couldn't see any of Galen's or Heath's men amidst the devastated remnants of the trail.

Within another minute the earth stopped sliding, but it took another five before Mike and Brock ventured on to it. And as they climbed, they saw the devastation Galen's men had wrought.

Compton had now emerged from hiding and was picking his way across the wrecked trail, but as he was more concerned about avoiding slipping than watching out for another ambush, Mike judged that Galen had gone.

Compton confirmed this when they reached him and he also confirmed that a combination of the explosions and Galen's ambush had decimated their ranks. Three men had received fatal gunshots, the second fallen tree had crushed another, and four, including Patrick, had been swept away.

Tyrone and the gold-wagon had gone.

The survivors: Compton, Mike and Brock stood in silence a moment. Confronted by the carnage, Mike felt numb, the shock deadening any uncomfortable feelings he might have about standing beside men who had stood by while Lazarus had staked him out to die.

Brock was the first to speak.

'I don't understand what happened,' he whined.

'Galen stole our gold,' Compton muttered. 'What's not to understand?'

'What Tyrone was doing for one,' Brock sneered. 'He headed off when those trees came down.'

'Yeah, he headed off to escape from Galen.'

'Or to run me down,' Mike said.

'Enough,' Compton commanded. 'Stop wasting your breath when we don't know what happened. First, we look for survivors. Then, we get our gold back.'

Although Lucy had told Mike about Tyrone's past and Mike reckoned that he could have used the opportunity of Galen's ambush to steal the gold, he kept his thoughts to himself, preferring to see evidence before he voiced his concern.

But after ten minutes of searching, all doubt disappeared.

Mike found Patrick's body, lying half-buried in dirt at the bottom of the slope, the force of the landslide having bent his limbs into grotequely contorted shapes.

He sat by the body, fighting back a sudden pang of loneliness of a kind that hadn't hit him in years. Despite problems of his own and constant rebuffs, this young man had befriended him and saved his life, and now it was too late to repay him.

But when he dragged the body from the ground, he found that the pressure of the earth hadn't killed him and neither had a gunshot from Galen's men. Scythed across Patrick's throat was a deep cut, a knife-wound from a practised hand.

He had been killed in the same way as Holman Reynolds had been.

As the ramifications of this discovery hammered their way into Mike's mind, he swayed, his eyes closing and his heart thudding.

Although this could be a coincidence, Mike reckoned that was unlikely. He had assumed that Roscoe Woods had killed Holman, but this discovery meant it was more likely that Tyrone had killed him when he'd visited Entoro on his apparent search for Holman.

But the fact that Mike had killed an innocent man wasn't as shocking to him as an even worse realization.

When he found his voice, he beckoned Compton and Brock to join him.

Each man looked down at Patrick's body, their jaws set firm, but when they'd all muttered their respects, Mike pointed south.

'Tyrone *has* stolen the gold and I know where he'll go,' he said. 'It's this gorge along Snake Ridge.'

'How do you know that?' Compton asked.

'It's a long story, but Tyrone is heading there and Galen will follow him. And when Galen tracks him down, he'll have a base that's so perfect, he could hole up there for months.'

Everyone spoke up at once. Brock supported him. Compton questioned him as to what else he knew, but although Mike provided curt responses to each question, he couldn't voice his worst fear.

Lucy was in that gorge, and Tyrone and Galen were heading there right now.

14

After the ambush had decimated Lazarus Heath's men, the group needed only the shortest of discussions to decide what they should do.

They rounded up the horses that hadn't been swept away. Then Brock headed back to the miners' camp to rustle up help for an assault on Galen and Tyrone, while Mike and Compton headed down the slope at a steady rate which would let Brock catch up with them before they reached the plains.

On the downward journey a persistent rain set in, complementing Mike's distraught mood, and he hunched forward in the saddle as he fought back the worries that threatened to engulf him.

He'd killed an innocent man. And an innocent woman, whom he cared for, was in danger from the man he hated.

But with the resilience that had got him through the last five years, he fought those concerns away and concentrated on his immediate task of following after Galen.

Brock arrived with reinforcements before sundown at a point about two-thirds of the way down to the plains. And with half of the miners — the most they could spare — riding in a trail behind, they hurried down the trail.

At no stage did they pick up either Galen's or Tyrone's trail, although the rain had been heavy enough to make that not too worrying.

Mike paid only scant attention to how everyone else was acting, but even so, after the earlier disagreements, he noted that Compton had taken control of the group and he showed no animosity towards Mike. And as Mike had helped him, Brock offered numerous supportive comments and the occasional apologetic muttering about his failure to stop Lazarus.

It was two hours after sundown when they reached the plains and Compton decided they should stop here.

Despite Mike's desire to ride on, he had to admit that this was sensible.

The next day they set off at first light, but by now a sickness had invaded Mike's guts. Even his ritual promise that Galen would be dead by sundown didn't cheer him, as the chances that they would catch up with Galen before he followed Tyrone into Entoro were now slight.

Despite the urgency the group maintained a steady pace that required minimal stops, eventually picking up several trails amongst which were the gold-wagon's wheel-tracks. Compton reckoned the tracks confirmed that Galen was pursuing Tyrone and, sure now that they were heading in the right direction, they followed them.

Mike hoped the tracks would veer away across the plains, or that he'd find Tyrone's body, which might mean Galen wouldn't head to Entoro, but

Mike felt increasingly that there was an inevitability to their direction.

As they closed on the gorge Mike relented from his silent brooding and let the others know he suspected that a woman was staying at Entoro. After this revelation sombreness descended on the group as each man prepared for the ambush ahead.

They were ten miles away from Entoro and the sun had set when Mike saw three riders approaching.

These men resolved into being Sheriff Beltran and his two deputies. Compton hurried on to meet them.

'Sure am glad we met you,' he said, 'for once. Galen Benitez has stolen our gold and we aim to get it back.'

'Has he?' Beltran said as he pulled up his horse, his lively eyes betraying his mirth at their misfortune. He ran his gaze over the miners before it rested on Mike. 'But you can stop doing my job for me now.'

Compton shrugged. 'We *can* work together. Lazarus is dead and I won't argue about who is in charge. The important thing is to get back the gold and help save this — '

'I don't care about that.'

'Then why are you here?'

Beltran gestured back at his deputies, who nodded, then drew their guns. As one, the lawmen swung them round to aim at Mike.

'I'm here to arrest Mike Donohue for the murder of Roscoe Woods.'

Mike winced as he ran his gaze along the row of lawmen and saw that he had no choice but to raise his hands.

'You got no reason to arrest me,' he said, trying to put as much hurt conviction into his voice as he could.

'I have. French Johannson recognized you. He wondered why you left the fight in the Paradise saloon. But I reckon you were avoiding the only person who'd seen you when you came to Last Hope and killed Roscoe.'

Mike gulped to moisten his dry throat.

'I wouldn't go back to a town where I

killed someone, would I?'

'Perhaps you would or perhaps you wouldn't, but either way, I got enough to take you back to Last Hope.' Beltran gestured with his gun for Mike to approach him.

'Hey,' Brock said, then nudged his horse forward to stand before the lawmen. 'We need your help to get back our gold, not to arrest Mike.'

'You don't order me around,' Beltran said, a smirk appearing. 'But if you don't move out of my way, I'll arrest you, too.'

Brock glared back, but then backed his horse, giving Beltran clear space between him and Mike.

'Listen to Brock,' Mike said, speaking quickly. 'You have to help us get Galen. I promise you I'll come quietly after we have him, but — '

'Ain't interested in your promises,' Beltran snapped. 'Throw down your gun.'

Mike moved his hand to his gun-belt, ready to unhook it, but then Brock ripped out his gun and blasted a warning shot in the air.

'Mike tried to save my life and I'll fight for any man who does that,' he shouted, backing his horse while still keeping the lawmen in his sights. 'He's coming with us to get Galen.'

Brock shot a glance at Compton, who also drew his gun.

The deputy to Beltran's right swung his gun round to aim at Compton, but Compton ripped off a shot that sent the man's gun wheeling away. As the other deputy wavered then threw his hands high, Mike drew his gun, then edged his horse sideways to draw alongside Compton and Brock.

Compton gestured to the lawmen to unhook their gun-belts. The deputies did as ordered, but Beltran needed a warning shot over his shoulder before he threw down his gun.

Then Mike gestured for the lawmen to dismount. While Brock and Compton covered them he directed them to sit back against a boulder at the side of the trail, where he tied them up with thick coils of rope.

When their hands were secure, Mike took a backward pace and collected a knife from Brock, then hurled it as far as he could. The knife stuck into the dirt, point down.

'I guess that whatever problems you had with Lazarus have now passed on to Compton,' he said, 'but I don't want any of these miners to be wanted men. So, you can get yourself free, but it'll take you a while to crawl to that knife and come after us.'

Despite this gesture, Beltran sneered at Mike.

'You'll all pay for this,' he grunted.

In response, each of the miners rode past the tied-up lawmen and offered their own mocking comments. Then, with every man whooping like a warrior, the group rode off down the trail, but Mike stayed back to stand before Sheriff Beltran.

'And don't go thinking,' he said, 'that I'll escape. I've made sure you can get free, and you won't have to search for me. Once I've killed Galen Benitez, I'll hand myself in.'

Beltran returned a volley of curses, but Mike turned his horse and hurried after the others.

★　★　★

The group reached the gorge containing the ancient city of Entoro two hours after sundown.

They'd headed along the high ground so that they could look down into the gorge from above. Mike crawled to the edge to peer over the side. Down below was the cave where he had stayed for three months. As far as he could tell in the moonlight it was deserted.

Mike sighed with relief, a strange feeling overcoming him.

For the last five years he had yearned for the moment when he could kill Galen, but today he'd hoped that they'd misinterpreted the tracks and that Galen hadn't followed Tyrone here, because then Lucy would be safe.

He would still have to find Galen, and even when he did his impending arrest meant he couldn't start a new life with her, but that wasn't as important as knowing she was safe.

But as Mike's eyes became accustomed to the faint light at the bottom of the gorge he saw what he'd feared seeing the most: the wagon Tyrone had taken was at the bottom of the gorge. And standing beside it was Lucy's horse.

Mike's guts somersaulted.

She was here.

15

Mike darted his gaze around frantically, searching for where Lucy might be. Then he saw movement: two men emerged from the cave in which he'd previously stayed.

At a steady pace, these men walked round the side of the gorge. Mike saw them relieve two hidden guards at the entrance to the gorge.

When these guards returned several men joined them in the mouth of the cave before re-entering.

Mike now reckoned he knew what had happened at Entoro.

Tyrone had reached the gorge, hoping to impress Lucy with the gold, but before he could force her to come with him, Galen had arrived. And now, Tyrone would be dead, and Galen would have taken Lucy prisoner.

Mike shivered, then decided they had

to launch their attack immediately, before Lucy should suffer the fate that had overtaken the others who had been unfortunate enough to fall into Galen's clutches.

He gathered everyone around him. Barking his orders, he ordered two miners to go to the top of the winding path that led out of the gorge, blocking that exit route. These men glanced at Compton, but Compton nodded, then confirmed that Mike was the person most suited to deciding how they could launch a successful attack in this gorge.

Mike grunted his thanks, then sent half of the remaining number to surround the main exit from the gorge, ordering two of them to sneak up on the guards and subdue them quietly when the rest were in position. He positioned the remaining miners at various vantage points from where they could look down at the cave, ensuring that they could keep Galen's men pinned down.

Then, with Compton and Brock

flanking him, he headed down into the gorge, taking a slow and winding route in the moonlight.

Closer to the cave, Mike saw a fire glowing in the entrance and heard subdued conversation, but it was low and contented. He didn't hear a woman's voice, but whether that was good news or not, Mike didn't like to speculate.

He also saw that two more guards were flanking the sides of the cave, but these men frequently glanced into the cave and exchanged comments with the men within, their calmness suggesting they didn't expect an assault.

As he'd heard no gunfire Mike assumed that the miners had knocked out the guards at the entrance to the gorge, so he ordered Compton and Brock to climb up each side of the cave to gain positions above the guards.

As they crept off Mike knelt facing the cave, ready to start the assault if they didn't get a quiet drop on the guards, but both men jumped down and knocked out the guards with simultaneous and silent efficiency.

From the side of the entrance Brock waved down at Mike and, bent double, Mike hurried up to join him. Then he peered into the cave.

The cave was thirty feet across and consisted of a long chamber with a short, blind tunnel at the end.

From the entrance he could see into all corners except the side on which he was standing. He counted twelve men, sitting in a circle around the bags of gold. From their hunched postures and grunted comments Mike guessed they were playing cards and betting with the gold they'd seized from Tyrone.

But no matter how much he looked around the cave, he couldn't see Lucy.

He encouraged Compton and Brock to see the layout of the cave for themselves, then exchanged silent gestures with Compton on the opposite side of the cave. They agreed that the original plan of starting an attack from a safe distance was unnecessary and that they should position the miners closer to the cave and launch an assault now.

Brock set off into the darkness to round up the miners, leaving Compton and Mike to settle down and wait.

Five minutes passed. Then a delighted cry echoed in the cave as the winner of the latest gambling round regaled everyone with a tale of his success and skill.

'Hey, Slim,' that man shouted, 'come and see what I've won.'

Mike gritted his teeth, guessing that Slim was one of the guards, then he glanced into the darkness, trying by the sheer force of his staring to speed Brock and the miners in their return.

'Hey, Slim, what you doing out there?' another man persisted.

Grunts and catcalls, then obscene suggestions as to what Slim was doing were voiced. Then footfalls paced to the entrance.

Mike and Compton stood back, melting into the shadows.

A man appeared in the cave entrance, his hand to his brow as he looked out then headed towards them. As, on emerging from the brightness of the cave, he wouldn't be able to see them immediately, Compton edged forward. When the man walked by he lunged for him. He wrapped an arm around his throat and pulled him back, but as the man bent backwards, a strangulated screech escaped from his lips.

As Compton clubbed the man unconscious Mike wavered, hesitating over whether to wait for the miners or to take on Galen, but then Galen barked out an order inside.

Hearing Galen's voice was all the encouragement Mike needed.

He threw himself around the side of the entrance and pounded inside, darting his gaze into all corners of the cave. Before him was the circle of men, but in the main bulk of the cave there was nobody else.

Then he fired on the run.

Several men stood between him and

Galen and his first volley of shots scythed through these men, wheeling two of them away. But then the rest regrouped and returned fire.

Mike hurled himself to the side, falling over a shoulder as he flopped to a halt, landing on his belly. Then he carried the roll onwards, slugs tearing into the ground behind his tumbling form, to hide behind the only cover within the cave: the flat boulder on which he'd recovered from his injuries after his previous encounter with Galen.

With his back resting against the boulder he reloaded, then jumped up.

Gunfire ripped around him, the shots ricocheting off the walls and cascading all around him. Still he couldn't get a clear shot at Galen, but he did shoot another man before he again threw himself to the ground.

Standing at the other side of the cave, Galen ordered his men to get him, his voice seeming to be only feet away in the confined space.

Then footfalls pounded as two men surged across the cave, seeking to outflank him.

Mike listened to their approach, waiting for the best moment to take them on, but then rapid gunfire exploded, the shots blasting into all corners of the cave.

As bullets whined and whistled around him, the puffs of smoke drifting away from the walls, Mike risked a glance.

In the entrance he saw Brock and a line of miners. They were using just the cover of their sustained fire to pepper the cave with a hail of bullets. Despite the fact that Galen's men were trapped and could never survive this onslaught, Mike found no satisfaction as he listened to their cries of pain and their rare bursts of return fire.

He had waited for this moment for so long, but even as he anticipated the moment when Galen cried out, his thoughts returned to the worst thought of all — what had happened to Lucy?

She had to be here, but if she wasn't Galen must have killed her. Although his imminent arrest meant he had no chance of a life with her, knowing that she was dead destroyed his anticipation of Galen's death.

Then the gunfire petered out.

Mike looked up. Bloodied bodies lay everywhere, sprawled with hunched postures or slumped against the cave walls, but on his first look he didn't see Galen. He was starting to count the bodies when Brock called from the entrance.

'Galen hightailed it down that tunnel,' he shouted, pointing at the short tunnel at the end of the cave.

Mike nodded. 'It goes nowhere. He won't get away.'

Brock rolled to his feet. 'You want help?'

Mike jumped to his feet and glanced at Brock for long enough to shake his head. Then he ran to the tunnel.

He pressed himself flat to the cave wall beside the tunnel. It was fifteen feet long. The light from the fire illuminated a stretch of wall for half its length, but Galen was hiding further in than that and Mike couldn't see him.

By the entrance Compton and several miners were edging from side to side to try to see down the tunnel, but Mike gestured at them to take cover. They ignored him, but a shot from the tunnel sent them scurrying for safety.

'You're in there, Galen,' Mike said. 'And I've got you pinned down.'

'I am in here,' Galen said, his tone mocking and confident despite his hopeless position.

'I've always promised myself that you'll be dead by sundown. I'm a few hours late today, but that don't matter. You won't see another day.'

'Quit gloating and come in here.'

Mike stood tall, taking deep breaths while he pictured the tunnel in his mind. He'd been in the tunnel several times in daylight and could picture the spot where Galen would stand. He was a tall man and to avoid feeling as if he was in danger of banging his head, he would stand about four feet away from the back of the tunnel and to one side.

'You're a dead man, Galen. You always have been.'

'For a dead man, I enjoyed myself a-plenty, like I did with your wife.'

Mike ignored the words, relishing only that Galen's speech had confirmed that his guess was correct. He shouted another taunt, then waited for Galen to respond. When he did he threw himself into the entrance.

He just had time to see the solitary tall shape in the tunnel. Then he fired.

His first two bullets scythed past Galen's form, but the third tore into his arm.

Galen returned a shot, but Mike jabbed in a heel and threw himself in the opposite direction, the slug winging past his arm.

And then he had Galen in his sights.

He ripped two quick bullets into Galen's chest, slamming him backwards, but even before he'd hit the wall behind him Mike had hammered another shot into him.

Then he rushed forward, snaking down the tunnel and reloading as he closed on Galen. Before him, Galen slid down the back wall.

Mike had wanted to say many things as Galen breathed his last, but as he punched in the last slug, they weren't as important as ensuring that Galen didn't get a chance to worm his way out of receiving justice.

With his legs planted wide he stood over Galen and hammered lead into him, the lifeless body twitching again and again, but only when he was reloading did he realize that Brock was standing beside him and shaking his head.

'He's dead,' he said. 'You can stop.'

Mike pushed Brock away and continued to reload, but then calmness descended on him and he let his mind accept the fact that, in all the chaos, he still hadn't found Lucy.

He charged frantically out of the

tunnel and around the cave. He pushed the miners out of his way as he ran from body to body, but although he confirmed that all the men in the cave were dead, Lucy wasn't here.

And neither was Tyrone.

Then he slid to a halt, a terrible certainty overcoming him as to what had really happened here.

He barged past everyone, ignoring all offers of help, and hurried outside.

The moonlight was bright enough for Mike to see up the sides of the gorge, and he hurried on, heading for the highest cave in the gorge, the one in which he'd found Holman's body.

On hands and feet he scrambled up the side of the gorge. His injured leg ached with the strain, but he was heedless of how much noise he made, knowing that the chances of a sneaky assault were gone.

When he reached the entrance of that high cave he stood to the side, listening. From within he heard rustling, then the scuffling of feet.

The moonlight was at an angle that let him see into the cave and he could see that the mummified body of Holman Reynolds was still propped against the side wall. Then he jumped to the side to stand in the entrance. Within, he saw what he'd half-expected to see.

Tyrone and Lucy were standing in the middle of the cave. Lucy had her hands bound before her and a cloth gagged her mouth.

And Tyrone stood behind her, a knife pressed against her throat.

16

'Put down that knife,' Mike said, forcing himself to keep his voice level.

Lucy stared at him over the gag, her eyes defiant but pleading.

'You got me wrong,' Tyrone muttered. 'Lucy trusts me, and now that you've killed Galen we're leaving to pick up where we left off before you wormed your way into her heart.'

Mike raised his hands, then paced sideways into the cave.

'She can't trust you after you killed Patrick just to steal that gold.'

'But I stole the gold for her. You said I had nothing to offer Lucy, but you were wrong. I'll pave Entoro with gold for her, just as the legends said it should be.' Tyrone snorted. 'What can you give her?'

'Nothing like that, but she didn't come here to find a city with streets of gold, and that just proves you don't understand her.'

'Even now,' Tyrone grunted, 'you're trying to turn her against me.'

Mike took a deep breath and forced his voice to take on a calm tone that he didn't feel.

'Listen to yourself. You are the one who has turned her against you. You have a knife on her. If you love her, take that knife away.'

Tyrone glanced at the knife. His eyes flashed, perhaps in surprise that he really was pressing a blade to her throat. With a shudder, he drew the knife away, but then Lucy slammed her elbow into Tyrone's guts.

Mike launched himself forward, but with Lucy's arms being tied, her blow had come without much force and Tyrone instantly grabbed a firmer grip of her shoulders, then swung the knife up.

Mike slid to a halt when he saw that Tyrone could thrust the knife into her throat before he'd covered half the distance to them.

For long moments he stared at Lucy. She opened her eyes wide, urging him to do something.

To try to reduce the tension Mike placed his hands wide, then inched them in to his gun-belt. He let it fall to the ground, then kicked the belt away, but Tyrone still glared at him and Mike saw in his cold eyes a determination that Lucy would be his or nobody's.

Then a chill wind rustled around Mike's feet, growing in intensity until it howled into all corners of the cave, taking with it a swirling flurry of dust.

Then a hollow scrape sounded by the cave wall.

He glanced to the side to see that the gust of wind had knocked the mummified body of Holman Reynolds to the side. It was slipping along the wall towards the ground.

Lucy screamed, the sound tortured behind the gag and, as the body crunched to the ground, she went limp. Tyrone shook her, but she'd fainted.

With her legs buckling she slipped from his grasp to the ground.

As she flopped on to her side Mike broke into a run, then hurled himself into the air. He caught Tyrone around the shoulders and slammed him to the ground, where the two men rolled over and over each other.

They came to rest on their sides, where each man gained a grip of the other man's arms. The knife arced back and forth between them. The blade caught stray beams of moonlight as the point arced towards Tyrone's chest, then to Mike's neck.

Tyrone managed to wrestle himself on top, but Mike kicked his legs up and tumbled him away. Then they were rolling again.

They strained for supremacy, Tyrone again getting on top. Dust clouded around them as each scuffed and battled to turn the knife on the other man. Then Tyrone rolled his shoulders and bore down, the knife edging inexorably towards Mike's neck.

In desperation Mike went limp, then wrenched his head to the side.

The knife plummeted, nicking Mike's left ear before the point clipped into the ground, sending up a brief spark. With Tyrone off-balance Mike slugged his jaw, sending him reeling. As Tyrone fell back he slashed out. Mike jerked his head back but the knife still slashed his cheek.

Now free of Mike, Tyrone rolled away, but Mike didn't give him a chance to get his bearings. He hurled himself on the tumbling man, encouraging his roll until they slammed into the back wall of the cave. In this position he trapped Tyrone against the wall and the two men stared into each other's eyes.

But then Tyrone's eyes rolled up and his head arched backwards.

Mike pushed himself away and saw that when they'd slammed into the wall the knife had buried itself to the hilt in Tyrone's guts.

Mike rolled to his feet and hurried to his gun-belt. He slid to a halt beside it and drew his gun then sighted Tyrone down the barrel.

'Time to give up,' he muttered.

Tyrone grunted his refusal and stared at Mike with defiance in his pain-racked eyes. He wrapped his hands around the hilt and tugged, but then screeched and fell back against the cave wall.

With his breathing shallow, he looked at Lucy. Then he shot out a bloodied and shaking hand and rocked it from side to side, perhaps pretending that he was touching her supine form.

But then the hand fell to the ground and his eyes glazed.

Mike knelt a moment, confirming that Tyrone was in no state to pose a threat.

Then he was free to go to Lucy.

★   ★   ★

Two hours after winning the battle in the gorge everyone grouped outside the lower cave while they awaited Sheriff Beltran's arrival.

Compton and Brock sat back, holding the men who hadn't died as their prisoners, while the other miners patrolled around them, although they didn't stray far from the gold.

Tyrone was still alive and sat with the prisoners. When Lucy had come to, she had balked at tending his wound, but her natural healing instinct had taken over. She had bound his chest and ensured he would live long enough to pay for his crimes.

Then, after exchanging short congratulations with Compton and the others, Mike sat with Lucy at the entrance to the lower cave.

Despite her terrible experience, Lucy was calm, but she clung on to Mike in a way that suggested she now understood why he had had to pursue an evil man until he'd killed him. But, more important, she was glad he'd also returned to save her from a man who was more misguided than evil.

Mike didn't mention that these were the only moments they had; instead, he concentrated on the simple pleasure of holding her.

The first hints of light were touching the eastern horizon when those moments ended: Sheriff Beltran arrived with his deputies riding behind him.

The lawman pulled his horse up at the bottom of the gorge below the cave and barely glanced at the sprawl of bodies and prisoners before he fixed his gaze on Mike.

'Mike Donohue,' he roared, 'it's time to keep your word.'

'I wasn't lying,' Mike shouted down at him. 'Just give me a minute. Then I'll come.'

Mike turned away, not giving Beltran a chance to argue. He flashed Lucy a smile, but she returned an open-mouthed stare.

'What did he mean?' she asked.

'I got to go.'

'But you came back for me. Galen is dead. You got no reason to do anything but . . . '

Mike put a finger to her lips, silencing her.

'Roscoe Woods is dead, and Sheriff Beltran reckons I killed him.'

Lucy shook the finger away.

'But that's ridiculous. You're a good man and you had no reason to kill him. I'll come with you and speak up for you.'

Mike put a hand on her shoulder and stared into her eyes.

'Please don't. I'll take my chances in court.'

Lucy threw herself into his arms and held on.

'I don't care what you say. I'm coming with you.'

Mike knew when he should give up on an argument and he held on to her as they walked down from the cave. His guts rumbled as he agonized over whether to tell her the truth now or later, but knew that he might never be able to say the words that would disappoint, and perhaps destroy her.

At the bottom of the gorge he planted a firm kiss on her forehead then removed her hands from him and stood before Sheriff Beltran.

'I said I'd give myself up. So, if you reckon I killed Roscoe Woods, I won't give you no — '

'Wait, Sheriff,' Tyrone yelled from the tangle of prisoners, his voice hoarse.

Beltran glanced away from Mike.

'What's wrong with you?'

With a hand clutching his bloodied belly, Tyrone looked up at the sheriff.

'You're here to arrest Mike for killing that no-good runt, Roscoe Woods?'

'Yeah.'

'Then you got it wrong.' Tyrone took a shallow breath and provided a sneer. 'I killed him.'

Beltran raised his eyebrows.

'You're confessing?'

'Tyrone,' Mike said, 'you don't have to volunteer anything.'

As Tyrone flashed Mike a warning glance, Beltran raised a hand.

'Why did you do it?' he asked.

'Roscoe had figured out that I'd killed Holman, so I had to dispose of him.' Tyrone shrugged, the action dragging a wince from him, then turned to Mike and mouthed something.

Mike wasn't sure what he said, but he guessed it might have been: 'Look after Lucy.'

Mike opened his mouth, but as he was about to refuse Tyrone's offer to take the blame, Lucy placed a hand on his shoulder and gripped it.

'So, this is over,' she said. 'And Tyrone will receive proper justice.'

Accepting that, in a way, she was right, Mike laid his hand on hers and watched the lawmen surround Tyrone.

For the next hour, Sheriff Beltran paraded around Entoro, muttering his displeasure at Mike's treatment of him. But eventually the realization hit him that Galen Benitez's bandit gang had been eliminated, and so he relented from carrying out his threat to arrest anyone responsible for his bushwhacking.

When he'd taken charge of the prisoners the miners embarked on a round of backslapping.

Mike exchanged his last words with

Compton and Brock, and refused an offer of work the next time they had to get gold out of the mine. Then he watched the miners leave with Sheriff Beltran to take the bodies and prisoners to Last Hope, and the gold to Green Springs.

Tyrone didn't look at Mike again, but as Beltran led him away he looked at Lucy for the last time, a terrible yearning in his gaze that said he would do anything to make her happy, and perhaps a hint of pride that in the end he had.

And then he was gone and Lucy and Mike were on their own in Entoro.

'Have you finished here?' Mike asked.

'I still have drawings to do, but perhaps I should leave them for someone else to complete.' She smiled as Mike grunted his approval. 'But I still have to ask — what do we do now?'

Mike sighed. 'I could ask you the same.'

She paced round to look up the gorge

towards the highest cave.

'I'll leave Holman here. He'd have wanted that.' She placed a hand to her heart. 'But I can't help but think about what happened in the cave. Tyrone was all set to kill me, but then . . . then Holman's body fell over and . . . '

'And you're asking me if his body fell over at just the right moment to distract Tyrone for a reason other than the wind?'

'Doesn't that worry you? Did Holman help me from whatever place he's in now? Did he try to tell me something about . . . about us?'

Mike glanced at a boulder and at the swirling pattern on it, then laid a hand on her shoulder.

'I guess that's the trouble with the dead. You never know what they want.'

'I guess.' She looked up at him. 'So, what's the answer?'

'You look into your own heart and decide what you want to do.'

Lucy patted his hand.

'I already know that.'

'Then come on. We got no reason to stay here no longer.'

They exchanged a quick hug. Then they left Entoro.

With their heads high they led their horses towards the exit to the gorge, where they stopped a moment.

One last time Lucy looked to the high cave, while Mike put a hand to his brow and watched the distant forms of the other men who were leaving this place.

He noted that amongst these men was the body of Galen Benitez.

Then they turned to the east and, as they picked their own route out of the Cauldron, the rising sun warmed their faces with the promise of a new day.

THE END

We do hope that you have enjoyed reading this large print book.

Did you know that all of our titles are available for purchase?

We publish a wide range of high quality large print books including:
Romances, Mysteries, Classics
General Fiction
Non Fiction and Westerns

Special interest titles available in large print are:
The Little Oxford Dictionary
Music Book, Song Book
Hymn Book, Service Book

Also available from us courtesy of Oxford University Press:
Young Readers' Dictionary
(large print edition)
Young Readers' Thesaurus
(large print edition)

For further information or a free brochure, please contact us at:
Ulverscroft Large Print Books Ltd.,
The Green, Bradgate Road, Anstey,
Leicester, LE7 7FU, England.
Tel: (00 44) **0116 236 4325**
Fax: (00 44) **0116 234 0205**